Praise for Chloe Aridjis

Guggenheim Fellow
Prix du Premier Roman Étranger Winner

"A young writer of immense talent." —PAUL AUSTER

"Chloe Aridjis is, for my money, one of the most brilliant novelists working in English today."
—GARTH GREENWELL

"*Sea Monsters* by Chloe Aridjis is destined to be a classic: a richly imaginative, reflective, and mesmerizing novel set in Mexico."
—XIAOLU GUO

"[A] young writer who see[s] the world with a fresh, original vision."
—WENDY LESSER, *The New York Times Book Review*

"Chloe Aridjis is crafting a poetics of the strange... this is deft and shimmering fiction."
—*The Times Literary Supplement*

"Hypnotic. . . . Aridjis' novel has the power of dreams and still hasn't left me."
—JUNOT DÍAZ, *Salon*, on *Book of Clouds*

"A post-Sebaldian, post-Benjamin peripatetic meditation. . . . One of my favorites this year."
—ALI SMITH, *The Times Literary Supplement*,
on *Book of Clouds*

"Exquisitely written. . . . A perfect story for our unsettled times." —FRANCISCO GOLDMAN on *Book of Clouds*

"Chloe Aridjis writes with a fine-tuned sensitivity and a captivating charm. Her universe is offbeat, rich, and disturbing in equal measure—but always utterly compelling."
—TOM McCARTHY

"Chloe Aridjis's gifts for narrative, description, and detail signal the arrival of a promising new writer."
—FRANCINE PROSE

"I am very excited by Chloe Aridjis."
—JEANETTE WINTERSON

"Chloe Aridjis writes about sensations at the edges of perception, capturing experiences rarely included in fiction. A surprising sensibility and an effortlessly original voice."
—EVA HOFFMAN

"Brilliantly exact and disconcerting. . . . Reading [Aridjis] is absorbing and enlarging to the imagination."
—DIANA ATHILL

Sea Monsters

ALSO BY CHLOE ARIDJIS

Book of Clouds
Asunder

SEA MONSTERS

A Novel

Chloe Aridjis

Catapult  New York

Copyright © 2019 by Chloe Aridjis
First published in the United States in 2019 by Catapult (catapult.co)
All rights reserved

ISBN: 978-1-936787-86-9

Jacket design by Strick&Williams
Book design by Wah-Ming Chang

Catapult titles are distributed to the trade by Publishers Group West
Phone: 866-400-5351

Library of Congress Control Number: 2018950155

Printed in the United States of America
10 9 8 7 6 5 4 3 2 1

J'ai rêvé dans la grotte où nage la syrène.

I have dreamed in the grotto where the mermaid swims.

GÉRARD DE NERVAL

Nocturno mar amargo
que circula en estrechos corredores
de corales arterias y raíces
y venas y medusas capilares.

Bitter nocturnal sea
that flows through narrow corridors
of corals arteries and roots
and veins and capillary jellyfish

XAVIER VILLAURRUTIA

Sea Monsters

IMPRISONED ON THIS ISLAND, I WOULD SAY,
imprisoned on this island. And yet I was no prisoner and
this was no island.

During the day I'd roam the shore, aimlessly, purpose-
fully, and in search of digressions. The dogs. A hut.
Boulders. Nude tourists. Scantily clad ones. Palm trees.
Palapas. Sand sifting umber and adrenaline. The waves'
upward grasp. A boat in the distance, its throat flashing
in the sun. The ancient Greeks created stories out of a simple juxtaposition of natural features, my father once told
me, investing rocks and caves with meaning, but there in
Zipolite I did not expect any myths to be born.

Zipolite. People said the name meant "Beach of the Dead,"
though the reason for this was debated—was it because of

the number of visitors who met their end in the treacherous currents, or because the native Zapotecs would bring their dead from afar to bury in its sands? Beach of the Dead: it had an ancient ring, ancestral, commanding both dread and respect, and after hearing about the unfortunate souls who each year got caught in the riptide I decided I would never go in beyond where I could stand. Others said Zipolite meant "Lugar de Caracoles," place of seashells, an attractive thought since spirals are such neat arrangements of space and time, and what are beaches if not a conversation between the elements, a constant movement inward and outward. My favorite explanation, which only one person put forward, was that Zipolite was a corruption of the word *zopilote*, and that every night a black vulture would envelop the beach in its dark wings and feed on whatever the waves tossed up. It's easier to reconcile yourself with sunny places if you can imagine their nocturnal counterpart.

Once dusk had fallen I would head to the bar and spend hours under its thatched universe, a large palapa on the shores of the Pacific decked with stools, tables, and miniature palm trees. It was where all boats came to dock and refuel, syrup added to cocktails for maximum effect, and I'd imagine that everything was as artificial as the electric-blue drink; that the miniature palm trees grew fake after dusk, the chlorophyll struggling and the life force gone from the green, that the wooden stools had turned to laminate. Sometimes the hanging lamps would be dimmed and the music amplified, a cue for the drunks and half drunks to clamber onto the tables and start dancing. The shore line ran through every face, destroying some, enhancing others, and at moments when I'd had enough reminders of humanity I would look around for the dogs, who like everyone else at the beach came and went according to mood. A curious snout or a pair of gleaming eyes would appear on the fringes of the palapa, take in the scene, and then, most often, finding nothing of interest, retire once more into darkness.

Before long, it became apparent that the bar in Zipolite was a meeting place for fabulists, and everyone seemed to concoct a tale as the night wore on. One girl, a painter with cartoon lips and squinty eyes, said her boyfriend had suffered a heart attack on his yacht and been forced to drop her off at the nearest port since his wife was about to be helicoptered in with a doctor. In more collected tones, a tall German explained to everyone that he was a representative of the German Society for Protection Against Superstition, or Deutsche Gesellschaft Schutz vor Aberglauben—he wrote the name in tiny German script on a sheet of rolling paper for us to read—and had been sent to Mexico after a stint in Italy. An actress from Zacatecas no one had heard of insisted she was so famous that a theater, a planet, and a crater on Venus had been named after her.

And you, one of them would ask, noticing how intently I listened, what brought you here?

I had run away, I told them, I'd run away from home.

Are your parents evil?

No, not at all . . .
. . . I had run away with someone.

And where was this someone?

Good question.

And *who* was this someone?

An even better question.

But that was only half the story. I had also come because of the dwarfs. However fantastical it now seemed, I was here with Tomás, a boy I hardly knew, in search of a troupe of Ukrainian dwarfs. I say boy, though he was nineteen to my seventeen, and I say dwarfs, though I had yet to see them with my own eyes. In any case, if I stopped to think about it for more than a few seconds, the situation was almost entirely my fault. Calming thoughts were hard to come by, no calm, only numbness, as if stuck halfway through a dream, yet the realization didn't trouble me.

The palapa held out the promise of one thing while the animated conversation and gaudy cocktails delivered another, and once I'd had enough I would return to my hammock through the sifting black of the beach and watch shadows advance and recede, never certain as to who or what they were. Sometimes I would see Tomás walk past, his shadow easy to pluck out from the rest, and although he kept a certain distance I recognized him instantly, tall and slender with a jaunty gait, like a puppet of wood and cloth slipped over a giant hand.

At some point I would have to explain to myself and to any witnesses how it was that I had ended up in Zipolite with him.

He had started out as a snag, a snag in the composition; from one moment to the next, there was no other way of putting it, he had begun to appear in my life back in the city. And since all appearances are ultimately disturbances, this disturbance needed investigating.

I didn't even particularly like him at first; *intrigued* would be a better word. He was a sliver of black slicing through the so-called calm of the morning. I still remember most details, the pinkish light that spread over the street, painting the tips of trees and the uppermost windows, the shops closed, as well as the curtains on houses, and the only person I'd encountered within this stillness was the elderly organ grinder in his khaki uniform, seated on the edge of the fountain below the looming statue of David, polishing his barrel organ with a red rag before heading to the Centro. HARMONIPAN FRATI & CO. SCHÖNHAUSER ALLEE 73 BERLIN, read the gold letters down the side, but the organ grinder himself lived in La Romita, the poorer section of La Roma, though he always came to the plaza near my house to polish his instrument, preparing it for a social day outside the cathedral. None of his kind had ever been to Europe but they carried Europe in their instrument, their uniform, and their nostalgic, old-fashioned manner.

And it was as he sat there on the bench beginning his day that I saw another figure appear: a young man in black, tall and slender with a pale face and hair shooting out in twenty directions, who walked up to the *organillero* and held out a coin—I assumed it was a coin, all I saw was the glint of a small object transferred between hands—and continued on his way. The elderly man nodded in surprised gratitude; he was probably used to receiving alms when music was produced, not silence, and here, out of nowhere, first thing in the morning, had come this offering.

Despite having to catch the school bus at 7:24 I followed the new person as he hurried down streets parallel to the ones I normally took, past *mozos* sweeping the streets before their employers awoke and tramps curled up in the porticos of grand houses beginning to uncurl. But once he turned off into Puebla my inner map cried out and I swerved around and retraced my steps in a hurry, arriving just in time to board my bus at the junction where Monterrey meets Álvaro Obregón. The quiet of the streets vanished the moment I stepped onto this traveling ship of the wide awake, wide awake thanks to the gang of new wave Swedes at the back. There were four of them, three boys and a girl—sister to one—and they colonized the last row with their blondness and asymmetrical haircuts, always one tuft eclipsing an eye, and trousers rolled up just enough to reveal their pointy lace-up shoes, but above all they colonized the bus with their portable stereo, for they asserted themselves, communicated almost entirely, through their music—Yazoo, Depeche Mode, the Human League, Soft Cell, and Blancmange—and it was in this way, after the first glimpse of Tomás, that I was launched into the day.

In Zipolite the sun seared the sand, and the heat particles, free to roam where they pleased, dissipated in the air. Yet our Mexico City was situated in a valley circled by mountains. High-pressure weather systems, weakened air flows,

rampaging ozone and sulfur dioxide levels, basin geography: a perfect convergence of factors, said the experts, for
thermal inversion. Ours was a world of refraction, where
light curved, producing mirages, and sound curved too,
amplifying the roar of airplanes near the ground. And
each time an event in Mexico challenged the natural order
of things, often enough for it to become part of the natural
order, my parents and I called it thermal inversion.

Thermal inversion whenever a politician stole millions
and the government covered it up, thermal inversion when
an infamous drug trafficker escaped from a high-security
prison, thermal inversion when the director of a zoo
turned out to be a dealer in wild animal skins and two lion
cubs went missing. But the real thing existed too, and on
some days the air pollution was so fierce I'd return from
school with burning eyes, and everyone from taxi drivers
to news presenters complained about the *esmog* but the
government did nothing. The clouds over our city were of
an immovable slate, granite, and lead, and only the year
before, migratory birds had dropped dead from the sky—
exhaustion, the officials had said, they died of exhaustion,
but everyone knew the poisoned air had cut their journeys
short, lead in the form of dispersed molecules rather than
compacted into a bullet.

At first I thought thermal inversion was only possible in
the city, and then I thought it possible in Zipolite only in

the form of the Swiss biker in black leather—his movements constricted by his tight leather shorts and leather
vest, he spent all day drinking beer on the sand, his black
leather cap surely a magnet for heat, and never entered the
water. Yet I soon began dreaming of other forms of inversion, for instance if I could replace Tomás with Julián,
my current best friend. Yes, if Julián were there instead, I
might have more perspective, somehow, on the given situation, or at the very least a proper interlocutor, be it in
silence or conversation.

But Julián was back in the city. He was back in the city,
on the top floor of the Covadonga, that was his address,
the old Spanish restaurant near the corner of Puebla and
Orizaba. The waiters at Covadonga would have cut funny
figures in Zipolite, like penguins at the beach in their black
waistcoats and bow ties, and the imperturbable expression
of those who'd seen a great deal over the decades; the place
had been around since the 1940s and some of them, according to my father, had worked there since their youth.
On the ground floor was a large spread of tables where old
men played dominoes, on the first floor a restaurant, on
the second floor a dance salon. Julián lived on the third,
used for storage and visiting musicians. He'd become
friends with Eduardo, one of the waiters, and, having nowhere to go after deferring university and falling out with
his boyfriend, brother, and father, was offered the space
on the condition that he vacate whenever the owner, who

lived in Spain, came to Mexico, and for any trios or duos
or solo musicians who happened to pass through.

The top rooms contained an assembly of half-living objects:
fold-out chairs and tables, some in stacks against the wall,
a gas canister hooked up to a four-burner stove, its stark
metal frame like a vertebra, and a red cooler with the letters CERVEZA CORONA in blue. The back room had a cot,
where Julián slept under a pile of tablecloths, surrounded
by boxes of folded linen and fluorescent tubes. A defunct
disco ball, missing most of its square mirrors, hung from
the ceiling; the only light was the one that glowed through
the windows shaped like portholes. In these rooms I'd
spend many an hour with Julián and his stereo, a General
Electric that guzzled size D batteries. In one corner was
parked a guitar with Camel insignia, for which his mother
had smoked her way through two hundred cartons of cigarettes; with the coupons and a bit of cash she had bought
it for her son one Christmas. He seldom played it, however,
since he felt she had died for that guitar.

The Corona cooler was kept well stocked, usually with Sol
or Negra Modelo, and we'd sit back in the fold-out chairs
and paint the future, the details changing each time, as we
wandered side by side through a landscape of perhapses.
Perhaps he would become a sculptor or a rock musician.
Perhaps I would become an astronomer or an archaeologist. Perhaps he would partner up with the owner of

the Covadonga and one day inherit the place and its four floors. Several days a week I would walk over after school, especially when my parents weren't home, and sensed at moments that this was the closest I would ever come to having a sibling. Sometimes we'd carry two chairs out to the narrow balcony, from which there was a view of the spire and rose window of the Sagrada Familia, our neighborhood church, though like many city views ours was bisected at different heights by a tangle of telephone and electricity lines. If the day was rainy or overly polluted we'd bring the chairs back inside and listen to the radio. One station played songs from England and Julián kept the dial there, though every now and then he'd swivel it over to a pirate station that offered unofficial news, a quick reality check before we returned to our fantasies, and other times he'd slip in a cassette and we'd listen to the same track over and over, usually Visage's "Fade to Grey" or the Cure's "Charlotte Sometimes," and we'd stop talking and just listen, letting all that had sunken well up inside.

WHEN I WAS YOUNGER WE KEPT AN AQUARIUM, A slice of sea in a corner of my father's study. It lived half in shadow since the curtains were kept semi-closed—too much sunlight encouraged algal bloom—and anyway, night was when it came alive. Whenever I couldn't sleep I'd go sit and watch a hermit crab making the rounds and a clown fish zigzagging across the tank while others pulsed by in their silvery-blue waistcoats. During moments of extreme restlessness I'd be soothed by the fact that total inactivity did not exist, even at three in the morning there was something in motion, a plan being executed at the most micro of levels. Someone once said that the dream is the aquarium of the night, but to my mind night was the aquarium of the dream, with our visions framed within it.

And then came the moment when the last fish died. My mother standing over the tank trying to ladle it out with a green net. As I watched from a nearby sofa, all was unleashed and for an instant it felt like the entire universe was focusing on our home. The phone rang. A knock on the front door. The fax machine trilled. A caterwaul from our neighbor Yolanda's house. Dogs howled from rooftops. Klaxons and sirens in the distance. Everything spoke at once, a collective dirge for the dead fish.

Whenever I felt disheartened or defeated I'd recall my father's words, words he would repeat long after we'd stored the aquarium at the back of a closet and filled it with papers. Remember, he'd say, society is like a fish tank, only less beautiful to watch. The structure is not so different, however: here we have the shy fish who spend their lives hiding between the rocks, missing out on moments both important and trivial, then the gregarious types who crisscross the water in search of company or adventure, always on the move without knowing where they're headed, and then the curious ones who hover close to the surface, first in line for food but also first should any hand or paw plunge in.

Yet his words lost meaning before the ocean, here there was no visible order or structure, only one great matriarch, vast and indifferent as a cathedral. And that indifference had to be reckoned with, it had to be measured and addressed if there was to be any interaction between humans and ocean. From my first day in Zipolite I noticed the system of flags—green, yellow, and red, each signaling a different strength of current, a code imposed on the ocean's movements: the ocean produced waves and we responded with triangles of color that mediated between us, rising up like strange pointy flowers on tall poles in the sand. No farther in than your knees, some said, because like everything dead, this beach and its waves will try to suck you under.

I now imagined my parents plastering my image to lampposts, my face added to the missing-dog posters in our neighborhood. *Se busca Azlán. Se busca Bonifacio. Se busca Chipotle.* Each time I saw one I would fantasize about finding the animal—for the animal's sake, for the owner's sake, for the reward. But no image was permanent. These posters would start out vivid, inked with the owner's nervous expectation, but as the days went by the hope and color would be drained from them and one morning they'd be torn down by a man in overalls who went around removing expired notices. Some of the animals I recognized but others must have spent their entire lives indoors; I had a pretty good sense of most of the dogs in La Roma, many of whom were brought to the park to run, others taken out by the neighborhood dog walker. Other sights: a pair of Rottweilers jumping up and down behind the wire mesh of their gate, two dark masses springing as if on a trampoline, fiercely guarding the only territory they knew, and our local priest, who would change into sneakers at night and walk his white Maltese through the dirty streets.

The dogs in Zipolite may have been safe from city woes, yet all day long they wandered up and down the beach as if scavenging for something not provided by the landscape. They took the beach's temperature, gauged its mood, sussed out every new arrival. A ragbag of breeds, none were one solid color but rather a patchwork of two or three tones. Some had faces like masks, pure black interrupted by a tan snout or a set of golden eyebrows, others resembled wolves or oversized cats. One had a splash of German Shepherd though he was much smaller in size and nowhere near as regal; these dogs were more like courtiers, but even among courtiers there must be a king, and the leader of the pack, as far as I could tell, was this unabashed Shepherd mongrel, average in height but lofty in carriage, whom the others followed around and turned to for cues.

From early on I noticed the dogs didn't take to Tomás. They would avoid him and snarl when he came too close. Yet he didn't pay much attention, and when they first approached—after all, we were new scents on the beach— he yelled *¡Lárguense!* and kicked the air near their heads.

I'd often share my snacks with them, whatever I happened to have, which was never very much, and as a result the motley congregation would come sit by my side. How had I ended up in Zipolite preferring the company of these dogs to that of the person I'd run away with, I'd ask myself, while the sea continued to write and erase its long ribbon of foam.

AFTER THE FIRST SIGHTING, EACH MORNING I'D EX-
pected the scene to be replayed. There was the organ
grinder perched on the edge of the fountain with his
rag and instrument, but he sat alone and the red rag announced nothing new, it remained a piece of worn flannel
run up and down the sides of the organ. On my way to the
school bus I took parallel streets but saw no one, nothing,
outside the usual, nothing that hadn't been absorbed into
the daily sights and routines.

And then finally, ten days later, I saw him a second time,
near some local ruins. After the big earthquake three years
ago I was constantly on the alert for what would emerge
from them, and our neighborhood was a living archive of
the disaster. We had ruins and we had the people in the ru-

ins, the new inhabitants of La Roma's twilight zones who had slowly begun to occupy the collapsed buildings and mountains of rubble. They moved in with their menagerie of strays, spectral cats with faint meows and mangy dogs who'd spend hours pawing at imaginary food in the crevices.

As for our modest house, its simple anatomy had saved it. Other houses on our street, ones with more complicated structures, had tumbled within minutes, casualties of the quake that had its epicenter in the Pacific Ocean near the coast of Michoacán. Far away, a tectonic plate had decided to shift and with its shifting that Thursday morning it dispatched a telegram that swayed, toppled, and razed all we'd taken for granted. Yet our house had remained standing. The pictures went crooked, as did several pots in the kitchen, but the only permanent mark was one fissure that appeared along the living room wall like a fallen lightning bolt.

The pile of ruins on Chihuahua was one of the most dramatic expressions of collapse, its massive concrete slabs and shattered glass seeming to multiply and mosaic over time, and it was there that I saw Tomás again. I'd been on my way to the stationery store when I came upon two aging émigrés. Our local enigmas, they had fled a Europe in ruins to live, later, among our slightly more humble ones. I'd often see them at the VIPS diner on Insurgentes bent over their coffee and *molletes,* the woman with a hand on her purse and the man with a hand on his cane, as if ready to leave at the slightest prompting. That day they were accompanied by their ancient dog, whom they'd take on walks around the neighborhood, the man in his black beret—the street kids called him Manolete—and the woman in gray with her hair swept into an irreverent bun. Yet it seemed that this trio, dignified and decrepit, had run into trouble, for they'd come to a standstill and the dog lay with his hind legs splayed behind him. What was the problem, I asked, to which the woman pointed and said in a thick accent that he was having trouble finding his footing. No worries, I replied, and despite my hesitation I lifted the dog from the rear and held him up so the paws could find traction, not an easy task since even in the fanciest of neighborhoods the pavement was remarkably uneven, the result of our sinking city and the roots of trees battling out their subterranean existence.

As I crouched there assisting the dog, whose fur was short and bristly, a boot stepped down centimeters away, one boot and then the other. Ankle boots, turquoise blue with a black heel. I glanced up and saw with astonishment that this somewhat unconventional footwear was attached to the young man from the fountain. He was looking straight ahead and didn't pause, nor slow his pace, as he stepped around our little ensemble.

Again, I had a strong urge to follow but the dog was still relying on me to stand—I released him for a second but he immediately began to cave—and as the paws continued to resist traction I saw the figure nearing the corner, but what could I do, I'd embarked on a good deed and couldn't depart halfway. After several more minutes of struggle the dog finally managed to stand on his own. Once he was back on all fours the émigrés thanked me, though not as profusely as they should have considering what I had just sacrificed in stopping to help them.

JULIÁN WAS WITH ME WHEN I SAW TOMÁS A THIRD time, on an afternoon when the sky was uncommonly clear. A few factories must've been napping, or half the city's cars on holiday, and even the trees seemed aware of the change and looked more expansive, easing into relaxed forms before the air reverted to its grim chemistry. Instead of staying in the Covadonga, Julián grabbed his camera and tucked a couple of beers into his bag and we headed over to Álvaro Obregón. We loved the avenue's *camellón,* a long public walkway that bisected the traffic, its green wrought-iron benches and eloquent trees, their branches twisted into unlikely shapes as if from daily conversations with the wind. Up and down we'd stroll, taking stock of changes like city surveyors. A new record shop here, an intricate balcony renovated over there, further elevation of the pavement here and there and there, a rightward tilt and a shift in contours at the ruins on Chihuahua, and the only features that remained the same were the wide angles of street corners left over from the days when carriages needed to comfortably turn them. Sometimes in the early morning the émigrés would also visit the *camellón*, I'd see them on my way to school and sense they'd been awake for hours, as if still on a European clock. But what I loved most were the fountains inhabited by bronze sculptures of classical figures solitary or interlocked, caught up in dramas from long ago, blind to the thousands of cars speeding past.

Today the only free bench was across from the hospital, and we sat and took clandestine sips from our beers until the traffic began to thicken. Afterward we resumed our walk, neither of us paying much attention to where we were headed, and before long we ended up in front of the abandoned house on Plaza Río de Janeiro.

The earthquake had also left many mansions empty and in disrepair. Some were being squatted and others had a resident guard camping out in one of the rooms, the light of his candle visible from the street at night. Directly next door, meanwhile, showing more signs of life despite existing in similar limbo, would be a ruin. This particular house had lain abandoned long enough for anyone curious to have gone in to explore. I'd been inside several times with friends, it was the perfect place to smoke cigarettes and pose for imaginary album covers, and once someone had thrown a party and the entire house with its dozen rooms had glowed and crackled with life, until the police arrived, tipped off by the music and candlelight, and drove everyone out. There were plans to develop it, some said, grand plans drawn up by the municipal director general of Caos y Desarrollo Urbano, but for now it still belonged to us.

I followed Julián as he cut a path through the tall weeds that rose around the house like the soil's unbrushed hair and we paused only briefly at the open lock, corroded by countless rainy seasons and impossible to close. Yet it added to the thrill of trespassing, and we stuck to silence as we stepped into the front room. Clawlike branches groped their way through the broken windowpanes. Shafts of light entered through gaps in the walls, creating checkered patterns on the floorboards. On a rafter overhead, the resident doves, alarmed by our entrance, murmured nervously among themselves, and a few puffed out their feathers to look larger.

Julián had borrowed the camera from his father when he'd left home; at some point he would return it, or perhaps not, depending on whether they spoke again. A compact rectangle of stainless steel, it looked more like a long, thick finger than any device for recording images. The sort of gadget spies might use, or Cold War villains. Minox was its brand name, Julián informed me, as he began to document the beams, the doves, the cracks in the walls, even the dead flies that lay in tiny heaps on the floor as if someone had swept them up and then abandoned the task.

After capturing most of our surroundings Julián went to pose on the edge of a windowsill and asked me to photograph him. I thought of a Russian film I'd once seen— characters in a crumbling house, water dripping in from a punishing sky—and searched for redemptive angles within the surrender and neglect. At first he was tense, I kept telling him to relax, and only after humming to himself was he able to loosen his jaw and drop his shoulders into a more natural position. Through the viewfinder I allowed myself to admire him, his long lashes and craggy nose, and couldn't help lamenting the orientation of his romantic preferences.

The film was advanced by sliding the camera shut and then back open, a pleasing movement that presented the danger of compulsive picture taking; I had to control my fingers. Julián went to stand by the stairway and rested a hand on the banister. As I began to photograph this new pose, sleeves and trousers growing dustier after every encounter with a surface, his figure seemed to double. At first I thought it was his shadow but the contours didn't match up. I lowered the camera and there he was, the young man in black, standing on the stair behind him. Sensing a presence, Julián jumped aside.

We didn't hear you.
No, even after all this time the stairs don't creak.

He'd been upstairs, he said, his voice a bit deeper than I would have imagined, but heard movement and had come to investigate. At first he thought it was the doves, they seemed to be multiplying, but he then heard humans, too. He glanced at me, fixed his hair, then down at the Minox in my hand.

How did you get in? Julián asked, commenting that the lock, though broken, had still been in place. There are many secret entrances, he said, without explaining why one would need them. They discussed the state of the house, wondered how much longer it would stand without any sort of intervention. And while they spoke I casually studied him, deciding that the portrait from up close was even better than from afar: grayish eyes and tufts of hair in all directions, and a gap between the front teeth, surely excellent for whistling. He seemed older than me, by two or three years, and was unusually pale, not in the synthetic manner of the blond stars of Televisa but rather like a *güerito de rancho*. His face was very round, almost lunar, and more than anything he reminded me of someone handsome I'd once seen in a music video, not the lead singer but someone in the periphery, on a parallel plane. His clothes, a medley of black, were made of thick cotton, and gave off a strong smell of pot. What brings you here? I asked, realizing I had yet to say a word. He'd recently dropped out of school, he said proudly, and was now working part-time at a bookstore. Which one? A Través del Espejo, on Álvaro Obregón.

Name: Tomás. Tomás Román.

After a few minutes he ended the conversation, said he'd been in the middle of something and had to return to it. An unfinished joint, perhaps, unless there was someone upstairs with him. A dead end within an abandoned house—well, who would have expected the dialogue to run on for hours—yet it now felt as though we were the only ones intruding. Julián said, See you around, and I waved mutely, and we walked toward the door as the doves fluttered up and resettled into new configurations.

AFTER THAT AFTERNOON, I BEGAN WALKING PAST the abandoned house often. But I couldn't bring myself to go in, not on my own, and Julián didn't feel inclined to visit again, explaining that none of our photos had come out, the film hadn't been loaded properly, and he was too superstitious to return. So what could I do but walk past in the hope of a chance encounter, and during the hours at school add *Tomás Román* to the margins of my notebooks. I wrote *TR* in all its variations, the name blowing up genie-like as I tried out different scripts, cursive, feral and humdrum print, but after so many hours I'd tire of seeing those ten letters in the same order, ten letters with the same two vowels, ten letters that with repetition should have worked some manner of spell, yet instead lay silent, coffined, on the page.

Each class had its notebook, the teacher's words at the center and my own thoughts gargoyled in the margins. Center, margins, center, margins, my focus traveled between the two. Stay at the center, I told myself, stay at the center, but my eyes and hand would gravitate outward. In calculus class Mr. Rodríguez asked me what I was writing so intently, and laughed his sinister laugh when I quickly hid the scribbles with my arm. Rail thin (childhood polio) and famously short-tempered, Rodríguez taught various levels of mathematics. The more difficult the class, the more exalted he'd become, thrilled by the infinitesimal twists of calculus and how they made us suffer, and the moment we grasped something he would take it further, pushing our green minds as far as they would go, although few of us, he knew, would be able to accompany him to the end of the journey.

Mundane voices kept trying to anchor my reverie, gravity struggling against the flying carpet, and I resented them all, even that of Mr. Berg, my favorite teacher, who, sensing my distraction, began calling on me more often. I had studied French with him since ninth grade, when I'd learned the first words of the language, and had now moved with him into level four. He never revealed much about his past, only that in France he'd been a lecturer, had met his wife and emigrated to Mexico in the sixties. His face was from another continent and another era, with hooded wide-set eyes and thick lips and sloping eyebrows. And even more like my favorite actor, Peter Lorre, his expression could go within seconds from gentle to glowering to broken and for-lorn, the face of someone historically haunted, a face that seemed to carry in it several chapters of European history.

I clung to him, or to the idea of him, more than he ever realized. I sensed he knew how hopelessly adrift I felt there among the sons and daughters of industrialists and politicians, and the transient Americans whose parents worked for transnational companies. Mr. Berg represented something beyond them all. Our school, the Colegio Campus Americano, or COCA for short, was a fortress in the middle of Tacubaya. Long ago Tacubaya had been a rural idyll, the home of rich people and viceroys, we were told, but the colonial village had been urbanized, and eventually replaced by streets lined with stores selling car parts and horse feed. From the bus window I'd often see men sitting on barrels drinking soda while children and dogs played tag in empty lots nearby.

Now in the autumn of 1988 the final countdown had begun and each hour drew us mercifully closer to that June day of the crimson gown and quadrangle. Once I graduated I would never have to see the likes of Paulina again, clad in her Guess and Esprit, who said my Doc Martens were construction worker shoes—*zapatos de albañil*, she'd called them—nor her boyfriend, Jerónimo, whose father was a PRI politician who took him to see bulls being tortured to death every weekend. I preferred Chucho and

Ximena, whose father had won the lottery; in most eyes, their money didn't count, so they remained humble. As for me, most people knew that my father taught at a university, even if his subject and salary remained subjects of discussion, but few were aware of my mother's translation agency, or of my scholarship.

At school I'd had one close friend and a handful of semi-friends. But I tended to avoid the girls; in one way or another, the friendships were all-consuming but quickly consumed, and the moment the match was struck it hurried toward its extinction. Male friendships lasted longer, it was no mystery, there were fewer vibrations of the pendulum, and my one friend had been Etienne. Etienne was Mexican but his parents worshipped all things European. He was a hemophiliac and had often missed class, but when he was there we would always sit together in the green area by the pool, far from everyone. The son of a famous painter adored by politicians and the bourgeoisie, he would tell me stories of the famous people he'd met and the fancy places he'd been to, and spent much more time with grown-ups than with anyone his own age. Apart from me he didn't seem interested in his peers. Every now and then he'd be summoned from class and picked up by his father's chauffeur, or else bump into something sharp like the corner of a table and be rushed to the school infirmary for an injection. I often saw his peacock father in the newspapers, his aftershave almost rising off the page as he received honorary this and that. Yet from one morning to the next my friend was gone, sent against his will to boarding school in Switzerland.

One day in French class Mr. Berg asked us to choose a Baudelaire poem to analyze. As he spoke and wrote Baudelaire's name across the blackboard, starting straight but ending obliquely, I began to feel as though recently I'd been wandering under a distant star. That evening I leafed through *Les Fleurs du mal*, alighting on different poems, trying to decide which to spend time with, but once the book fell open at "Un Voyage à Cythère" I knew my attention would remain there. How did I know? Because Cythère was Kythera, it was one and the same place, that small legendary island off the Peloponnese that had caught the imagination of many painters and poets, and, more importantly, of my father. I didn't know which I preferred, the cackle of Kythera or the sorceress *C* of Cythère, but in any case, both designated the alleged birthplace of Aphrodite, or at least one of her birthplaces, since the exact site, like so much in myth, was contested.

In the opening verse the poet's heart is swooping about like a bird, free and happy around the rigging, but soon that buoyant spirit gets ensnared in gloomy pessimism and the poem ends with the macabre image of the sacrificed poet hanging from the gallows. It may start with a ship setting out under cloudless blue skies but the truth, at least in my interpretation, was that the poem's heart was a carbonized black, and Kythera a somber rocky place where dreams got dashed against its shores. When I told him which poem I'd chosen Mr. Berg said I'd made a good choice and then, cryptically, asked me to bear in mind that events were the mere froth of things, and one's true interest should be the sea.

The sea. Up until then, my father's only way of interesting me in the ancient world had been through shipwrecks. That was how he drew me in, made me feel occasionally connected to the ancient. Me, I preferred the modern, whatever it was, exactly, and although I listened as diligently as I could I tended to drift before long. Aeschylus and Sophocles had failed. So had Lucretius. Descriptions of pillar and tree worship in Mycenaean times. The spring configuration in ancient Chinese locks. Even descriptions of the design of chariots in ancient Egypt, the poles and the axles, dismantled at the funerals of pharaohs in order to negotiate the narrow corridors of tombs. Facts gleaned from conferences rather than from the books in his study;

print couldn't keep up with the advancement, in his words, of historical minutiae. With my mother, conversation was open and emotional with little withheld, but with my father there was a constant search for paths of communication that led away from ourselves.

It was only after he attended a conference on corrosion studies, the long-term interaction of materials in marine environments, that he returned home and was able to reel me in. He'd begun by telling me about a metallurgical report someone had delivered concerning a section of corroded candlestick from the *Gilt Dragon*, a seventeenth-century Dutch vessel that had struck a reef and gone down off the coast of Western Australia. Interesting, yet not enough to last for more than one meal. But he then moved on to something more thrilling, enlivened by much more detail.

Shipwrecks fall prey to all sorts of appetites, he said, the appetite of salt water, the appetite of sea creatures, the appetite of time. In the Mediterranean there are three main saltwater macro-organisms that share a fondness for ancient timber: the shipworm, the wood piddock, and the marine gribble. All three contribute to the stratification and contamination of the wreck. These marine borers are able to endure even the harshest conditions and can adapt to nearly every depth. Water temperature and salinity are their main gauges.

Marine gribbles, more sonorously known as Limnoria, tunnel into the wood in pairs, with the female forging ahead. Sharp-clawed and seven-legged, they are found in most marine and brackish waters, often present in large numbers. The channels they create run parallel to the surface of the wood and tend to communicate, rendering an infested vessel even more vulnerable to corrosion. Though they roam freely, gribbles have hermitlike instincts, and are loath to leave once they're ensconced in the burrows they've created: why move home when you have a roof and an endless supply of wood, peace, and quiet?

The shipworm, meanwhile, is a bivalve mollusk without shell or gender that changes sex as it grows. Also known as the termites of the sea, shipworms are less endearing in appearance than gribbles, with long, slender bodies and heads that resemble gaping mouths in service of an insatiable appetite that incessantly combs the water. Their bodies become longer as they burrow, leaving a calcareous deposit in their wake.

And finally, the wood piddock. Unlike the other two, the piddock is unable to digest cellulose: it seeks out wood not for nourishment but as protection from whatever dangers the sea may present. Its burrows are shallow and spherical; it attacks in big groups. Like the shipworm, the piddock is bisexual, and similarly content to remain in its chambers once satisfactory lodgings have been found.

The job of these organisms is made easier, and the yielding of submerged wood therefore swifter, thanks to the handiwork of two micro-organisms, fungi and bacteria, who break down the tissue before the others come to dig their channels. Along with this array of wood-boring creatures and their lesser counterparts, wave action adds to the process of demolition. The movement of water, as well as the movement of the seabed as the sand shifts and resettles, furthers the toll on the sunken vessel.

How to ignore the tragedy of the wreck, like that of a carcass in a wildlife program, no longer breathing yet under continued assault—once the mortal blow is dealt, a host of scavengers moves in. But I also cheered for these aquatic hermits who had found a home. Listening to my father describe the scenario made me feel I had access to something vertiginously distant and mysterious and of the various wrecks he mentioned, his favorite, and soon mine, was that of Antikythera, which had lain at the bottom of the ocean for twenty centuries. For twenty centuries, the ship and its contents had remained at the mercy of tides, currents, organisms, and upwellings. For twenty centuries, they lay silenced.

AT NIGHT THE WAVES OF THE PACIFIC WOULD GROW tremendous, swelling in height and in volume, a maritime thunder outdinning every other gesture of nature, and I'd watch as surfers materialized on the horizon like rare mammals from the sea. Dogs would bark at them from the shore with their hackles raised, and I'd wonder whether we all fell prey to some form of coastal delirium, a delirium born from the potent alignment of air, sand, and sea; after all, a mere drop of water can interact with light in an infinite number of ways.

The first three sightings of Tomás were followed by none, so one afternoon when I was feeling fortified—three A's at school that day—I dropped by A Través del Espejo. As much as I liked the idea of it, I didn't go there often. The place was topsy-turvy, with erratically packed shelves and signs in different languages and piles of books rising from the floor to the height of children. Positioned at the till as if to contradict its chaos was the owner, a stern woman with a pageboy haircut; she never smiled, never helped, and expressed annoyance whenever someone inquired into the availability or location of this or that book.

I crossed paths with Tomás, nearly brushed sleeves, as I walked in. He was on his way out, accompanied by a couple around his age whom he introduced as the Americans. He was taking them to see an apartment, he said. Which apartment? I asked, wondering whether he was now working in real estate, too. The apartment where William Burroughs shot his wife, he said. These Americans had come into the shop asking whether someone would show them, could pay fifty pesos, and since Tomás had been there once before he volunteered, and got permission for a short break. Do you even know who Burroughs is? he asked me. Yes, I do, I said, though I've never read him. My mother had two books of his and every now and then, sensing they held something illicit, I'd peer inside, searching for incendiary words and scenes, but was always left feeling short-changed.

Moments later I was walking down the street with Tomás and the two Americans, the girl chubby and snub-nosed and exuding an impressive confidence, the boy somewhat timid and half her girth. Tomás led us to the corner where Chihualiua meets Monterrey, paused, then turned right on Monterrey and stopped in front of number 122, a gray building with a black door. It opened with a push. We entered the tiled hallway and climbed a chilly flight of stairs but at the first floor our steps were cut short by a floor-to-ceiling grate that blocked access to a whole section of the corridor. A woman in a tracksuit and flip-flops emerged from one of the apartments and asked what we wanted. We'd like to see— No, no, no, the woman interrupted, aware of where the sentence was heading. Number 8 was a private residence. After moving in she and her husband had put up this barrier because people kept coming by, Americans wanting to make a television series, Americans wanting to make a documentary, Americans wanting to do a photo shoot. The young couple pleaded. They said they were students from San Francisco who loved William Burroughs and wanted to see the place where it all happened, the place that made him a writer, the place that made him a different person from when he entered. The woman seemed moved. I could see her studying the eager couple, their Converse high-tops and woven bracelets from the market, and after biting her lip and glancing over at me and Tomás to make sure we weren't renegades, she finally said, Okay, five minutes, and unlocked the gate.

As far as I could tell, her home contained nothing foreboding apart from the walls being decked in Christmas decorations, with pots of poinsettia on the sills; it was unclear whether these were left over from the previous year or put out a few months early. The windows of the apartment looked onto an interior courtyard whose upper tiers were crisscrossed with laundry. The woman's husband surfaced from a side room. His jeans were fastened with a string and he spoke and moved in stutters as if he'd suffered a stroke. His wife told him why we were there, upon which he sighed, especially when the young Americans asked whether they knew where in the flat *it had all happened,* there seemed to be many spaces and they wanted to know which held meaning. The woman pointed to a piano in the living room, an old piano covered in doilies, nearly eighty years old, she said, no one ever played it but in its spot the lady was shot. With forensic hunger the American boy began to circle the piano as if the instrument had absorbed some of the drama from thirty-seven years before, and started taking photos from different angles, his camera clicking loudly each time he pressed down on the button and wound the film.

As he took pictures the woman positioned herself in front of the piano and her husband stuttered over to the arch dividing living room from dining room, and solemnly announced that here was where Burroughs himself had stood, under the arch, and taken aim. Husband at one end, wife at the other. Face-to-face. All movement halted as they set up the scene. Despite their earlier protestations I had the sense they had done this before, inviting friends over to pantomime the famous incident that had taken place under their roof. The seconds passed, taut and bizarre, as each of them stood in their places. I sensed I was being watched. Tomás was staring over at me. Lips curled, eyes slightly narrowed. I wasn't certain how to meet the expression so I smiled, but since his lips were already curled I couldn't tell whether he was smiling back. Well, he must be, I decided; perhaps he was thinking what I'd begun to think, that this was a space of couples, first Burroughs and Joan Vollmer, then the married pair who lived here, and the young Californians. And now, Tomás and Luisa. Three couples, albeit one deceased, and us. Different portraits of modern coupledom. Story of an Afternoon with Piano and Couples. Tomás returned his attention to the husband and wife, who continued with their pantomiming as the rest of us stood quietly in our places.

After a minute or so the American girl, now powdered-milk pale, brought the session to an end. Well, thank you, I think we've seen enough, she said softly, her hand tightening around her bag strap. It'd been too much, I sensed, she'd gotten more than she'd expected. Thank you, we echoed. The man waved from under the arch but his legs stayed rooted, unfreed from the spell. His wife accompanied us to the gate.

On our way out I noticed it was the rest of the building, rather than the apartment itself, which seemed to hold something of that unfortunate past. The hollowed steps, the cold, blue shadows of the stairwell. I was eager to return to the street but Tomás insisted we have a quick look at the patio at the back, an outdoor space enclosed by four high walls, home to a Cal-o-Rex boiler and a black door lying horizontal. It wasn't the original from 1951 but one of many reincarnations, Tomás explained; the past ten doors had been documented over the years by a fan. Up above I glimpsed a patch of blue beyond the hanging laundry and walls of blistered plaster, beyond the pleated curtains flapping in the windows like women's nightgowns pressed against the sills, restless and billowing and ready to leap out into this domestic void of the inner courtyard. In silence we headed back toward the street, through the corridor where light bled around the rim of the front door and pooled into long white bars on the floor tiles, and it was there, in these communal spaces, that one felt captive to the building.

Once back on the street the Americans handed Tomás a fifty-peso bill and disappeared into a yellow Volkswagen Beetle taxi. The last time he'd gone to the apartment, he told me with a note of disappointment, there'd been three sisters living there with their five parrots, as you can imagine it was a bit noisier . . . Well, anyway, thanks for coming, he added, he had to get back to work but I knew where to find him, and off he went, hands in pockets, reverting to a black streak.

• • •

Yes, he was intriguing, but he wasn't the only one. Later in my room I ran through my list. From nights out there'd been Tiburcio Pérez, an artist from La Quiñonera with long hair and amber jewelry who attached reddish brown scorpions, our city's native *Vaejovis mexicanus Koch*, to thickly painted canvases. La Quiñonera was an artist's colony in La Candelaria, through the rusted gate you'd step into a vast unruly garden and there, at the end, beckoned a large stone house with four entrances. It was always cold at night and many of the artists wore ponchos, ponchos and some manner of pendant, often a silver cross or an animal tooth. And of course there was pulque, a lot of pulque, buckets brought fresh from a faraway town, and we'd gather round and dip in our cups, the air pungent with the heady scent of copal, and the copal would merge with the smell of unfiltered Alas and Faros and Delicados, those were the cigarettes of choice at La Quiñonera. Someone would always be painting while someone else would be playing the guitar, others would be arguing over politics or philosophy in the kitchen, and there were dogs, dogs everywhere. After Tiburcio came Alfonso, an anesthetist by day and drummer by night. My father's greatest fear was that I would end up with a *rockero*, so this one time I stepped out with a musician set his hair on end, especially when I accompanied Alfonso to concerts to see howling monkeys, that's what my father called them, howling monkeys, although my drummer would never howl, he'd sit serious and tight-lipped, sweating profusely as he banged out his rhythms. I'd also liked one of the Swedes on the bus, by the name of Lars Karlsson. There were probably 100,000 Lars Karlssons in Sweden but only one, or a few, in Mexico. Lars appeared gentler and more approachable than the other Swedes yet I found it impossible to speak to him, and on the few occasions he ended up sitting beside me I'd spent the entire ride trying to think of something to say. And then there was Andrés, who liked kicking boxes, he'd kick any box he found lying on the street; because of his deranged expression my mother had him drive her around the block a few times before allowing him to take me to the movies. There would also be the random boy from school I would dream about and the next day in class feel a connection to; after all, if he had gatecrashed my dream there must be a reason, especially when I'd hardly noticed him before. It would always be an individual from whom I would never have expected interest in either direction, usually preppy, with brown loafers and light pink button-up shirts; whereas I dressed almost entirely in black and would pin up my hair in extravagant ways. Yes, it would've been a shock if one of them had turned around and asked me out, indeed shattered all preconceptions, and yet my dream, so vivid, had introduced a thin crack in an otherwise impenetrable surface, and at first I'd wait for some sign of acknowledgment. But no, there'd be none, not even a glance, and over time I would have to accept that the dream bore no message, there was no connection, and once more the random boy would fade into the background, to become simply another face in the classroom.

As for Tomás, yes, he had been a snag in the composition, somehow inserting himself in the picture in a way the others had not.

ON DAYS OF LESS POLLUTION ONE COULD SEE THE volcanoes there on the edges of our city, taunting and majestic, their contours carved by light, their slopes scaled by countless imaginations, even mine, especially at moments when I felt hemmed in. Needless to say, there were still plenty of scenes and vistas of which Tomás did not form part. Not even as an idea. It was important to have those too, and the most successful of these intermissions was an evening spent at the home of my friend Diego Deán, punk rock singer, draftsman, and occasional shaman.

A small gathering, he'd called it, which it was in size but not tenor, our festivities conducted under the gaze of his three iguanas, who blinked warily each time a new guest arrived. Diego had produced hundreds of sketches, from all angles and perspectives, of his companions: frontal, profile, rear. He drew their prehistoric eyes, their lazy lids, their heavy blinks. These sketches hung on the walls between the bookshelves, and it was hard to tell where his pride lay most, with the drawings or the pets.

That night the creatures had watched us from their enclosures, tall glass tanks that loomed over the furniture in the living room. Someone put on a Klaus Nomi record while a large spiral of white powder was prepared on the coffee table, cards angled left and right creating whorls so thick it looked like the ghost of an ammonite, a logarithmic spiral like the ones from last year's geometry class. Once the spiral was completed Diego rolled a fifty-peso note into a cylinder and helped himself to approximately two centimeters of powder. After inhaling he passed the note to the guy next to him, who repeated the action before passing it on. Eventually the rolled-up banknote reached me, its paper warm from so many fingers, and what could I do but join in the ritual.

The bold hum of voices, mostly male, rose and fell around me, everyone talking and thought-walking like Cantinflas, their voices expansive, compulsive, filling every inch of air. And soon I too felt charged, charged and restive and impervious to everything, and after two lines I rose from the sofa and marched over to one of the iguana tanks and stuck in my arm. But scarcely had my fingers touched the top of the scaly head than Diego rushed over and yanked my sleeve, saying I'd clearly never experienced the dinosaur teeth or dinosaur scratch or dorsal thwack of their tails, not to mention one should never approach an iguana from above, only from the side, otherwise they think they are under attack, and furthermore, it takes years to gain an iguana's trust, he said with pride as the creature looked up at us with an indifferent eye.

Diego returned to the table, circling the spiral like a sinister jester. Someone turned up Klaus Nomi and for a moment the living room was transformed into an opera set and in my mind Diego Deán and Klaus Nomi became one. Diego could be Nomi without the makeup, it occurred to me, they had the same arched eyebrows and beaky nose and rosebud mouth. Then again, Nomi had recently died of AIDS in solitary conditions in New York, I remembered reading, people too scared of the new disease to even visit. Dark thoughts began to wash over me, the shadow side of drugs, which was why I didn't venture there often, and I tried to sink into the sofa despite being too wired to properly sink, observing the dwindling spiral as every few minutes another whorl vanished, every guest part of the anti-helical operation that slowed down as we neared the center.

I'd been thinking of getting up and checking on the iguanas when the doorbell rang, announcing the Afterhours gang. They were like astronomers: night was never long or black enough. First there was Cera, who with his 1940s suit and ruddy cheeks and greased-back hair reminded me of a wind-up doll, and his sidekick El Chino, who lived with his pet canary, Juan El Ciego, blind since birth, for whom he fashioned nests out of discarded shoulder pads. And El Chino's older girlfriend, Lorita, a tense woman in a purple jacket who had a habit of finishing other people's sentences. And last, El Pitufo, a coke dealer who wrote poetry; people listened to him recite his latest poems in exchange for free samples, and the more they consumed, the better his poetry sounded to their ears. He longed to be taken seriously, but when people saw him all they could think of was fine white lines.

Another spiral quickly formed on the coffee table, cast forth from a folded white envelope rather than any mystery of torsion. El Chino replaced Nomi with Bauhaus, then Japan. The spiral changed shape, everyone spoke at once, and whenever someone approached the table the others followed their movements with dilated pupils, rarely a pause between beers, words, or cigarettes, and that night I felt deliriously detached from it all. Detached, that is, until I began to worry about the iguanas. We were keeping them up; they looked increasingly vexed. I suggested we dim the lights and turn down the music but no one, including myself, could be bothered to tend to either, and only when an iguana nodded off, its dropping lid shutting

out our species for the night, did it occur to me to check
my watch, which read ten to three, information that jolted
me back to my senses, and I said goodbye to the sleeping
creatures and left the others to their fine white lines while
El Pitufo recited his. But once home, it was impossible to
drift off. A white electricity ran through me, as if my system had been rewired by an evil technician. Only then, as
I tossed and turned under my wool blanket, did I think
of Tomás, amazed that I'd completely forgotten about his
existence for nearly five hours, but now the technician had
returned those thoughts, and others, to their casing.

THE VELOCITY OF PARTICLES TRAVELING ALONG A given axis; the indispensability of horses and railways during the Mexican Revolution; a map of chromosomal deviations; character development in *Macbeth*. Evenings, once I had completed my other homework, I would return to the Baudelaire poem, trying to approach it from different angles to see whether a little more light might enter the landscape. And during the ten days that I worked on it, jotting down whatever occurred to me at whatever moment, I had a series of further encounters with Tomás that at times seemed to echo the poem's ambiguous message.

The Kythera from the poem was remote from the Kythera of my father's stories, yet in my mind the images began to

merge—as did the two islands, Kythera and Antikythera.
Yet each really did have its own wreck: the Kythira Strait
was one of the greatest navigational hazards of the Mediterranean, an infamous graveyard for shipping, a place of
sandbars, shoals, and sudden currents, my father would
quote. Kythera's shipwreck wasn't as famous or as ancient
as Antikythera's, though its cargo was. On board the ship
were some of the Elgin marbles, the ones Lord Elgin had
taken from the Parthenon. He was bringing them to England in 1802 when his ship the *Mentor* crashed into some
rocks and went down off the coast of Kythera. The salvage
operation began immediately and all the goods were re-
covered with the help of the locals, who were never told
what was inside the seventeen cases they brought to shore,
Lord Elgin insisting they contained nothing but rocks of
no value.

That was Kythera. But the Antikythera shipwreck belonged to the great canon of shipwrecks, my father insisted, and his enthusiasm was easily transmitted. The
vessel had been heading from Rhodes to Rome, it was
believed, when it went down off the coast of Antikythera
sometime around 70 or 60 BC, and lay on the seabed until 1900, when it was discovered by sponge divers from
Symi who were taking shelter in the bay from a storm.
The diver who first came upon the wreck thought he was
seeing a row of drowned men and horses lined up on the
sea shelf, and returned, terrified, to the water's surface.
But when the captain dived down to have a look he saw

they weren't men of flesh but of bronze and marble, in total thirty-six sculptures, men and horses, like the scattered pieces of a chess set. Along with these sculptures and a collection of jewelry and amphorae was a bronze mechanism, an astronomical instrument with more than thirty gears that could measure the movement of the cosmos, its fragments kept pressed together by the tremendous pressure of the water. Ancient clock, calculator, calendar, computer: archaeologists were still trying to figure out what it was, and decipher the inscriptions that covered its surface.

The Antikythera Mechanism. When I heard those nine syllables, I couldn't help thinking of the Baudelaire poem, envisioning a mysterious force that worked against the romantic, some sort of in-built mechanism that sprang into action whenever someone began heading toward Kythera, although the Kythera in the poem was far from idyllic. Without mentioning my theory, I described it to Tomás, this enigmatic feat of engineering that had survived against all odds, a bronze instrument found among the sunken treasures, if he liked abandoned houses why not vessels on the seabed, but he simply propped his feet on a chair and said, Well, I once found a five-hundred-peso coin at the bottom of a swimming pool, and pulled a face as if to say this wasn't the moment for scholarly matters. And perhaps he was right, for as we sat there in my local ice cream parlor La Bella Italia, right by the Wurlitzer

jukebox with its glowing eyes and silver-grille mouth, I
was struck by how quickly the thoughts that occupied my
mind at home became irrelevant once I stepped outside,
especially when face to face with someone physically al-
luring, there was no denying the fact, and as I looked out
onto the street, hectic and sooty compared to the parlor's
smooth, tidy interior, Tomás began telling me about how,
after dropping out of school, he'd gone to live with an uncle. He spoke of his uncle's house with its peculiar insects
and haunted furniture. I then told him about my father's
pathologically shy cousin Gamaliel, who would come over
to play chess. He seldom ventured out and had the awk-
wardness of someone who spent a lot of time on his own,
but was assertive on the chessboard and nearly always beat
my father. Tomás then told me about an aunt of his, an ob-
sessive gardener of cacti, although as far as he knew cacti
didn't require much gardening. This aunt lived in Satélite
with her husband and cat, a fluffy animal whose fur absorbed the cooking smells of the house. And as we spoke
about our relatives rather than ourselves I'd lower my eyes
and watch the ice cream in my dish losing its shape, what's
more part of the universe seemed less spherical than it had
only moments earlier, and then I'd glance up at the gap
between his teeth, speculating whether it was the sort of
detail one grew used to, eventually, and at moments our
questions and answers felt as random as the songs playing on the jukebox. In what way is your uncle's furniture
haunted? Oh, you know, it tries to hold on to me when I

stand up, it doesn't release its grip. I must've looked con-
fused since he quickly added, Speaking of which, why
don't you come with me to the wrestling, I'm going next
Thursday and have two tickets.

In order to go to the *luchas* I told my parents three lies.
First, I told them I was going to see a play. Then, that I'd
be with Julián and his (imaginary) cousin Miguelito. Last,
that the theater was in Colonia Cuauhtémoc. The truth
was, I was going to watch the *lucha libre* with Tomás at
the Arena México in Colonia Doctores, a neighborhood
known for car theft and delinquency, where grocers had
installed gates in front of their shops and conducted business through the bars. As far as I knew, no one from school
had ever been to the district or the wrestling.

A red sun sinking into a bronze sunset, colors as satu-
rated as those of artificial flowers, ushered us into the evening. Tomás grabbed my hand just as we were engulfed in
the stream of people pouring into the arena, a thick lava
flow driven by scorching anticipation. Inside, the atmosphere was as raucous as my father's descriptions of the
Roman coliseum—men, women, children, grandparents
filled the benches that surrounded the ring, a large quadrilateral rising from the center of the hall. We took our

seats in row 23 while the snack seller hurriedly made the rounds with bags of chips and beer in plastic cups. And then a torrent of raunchy music followed by the MC, a mustached man in a black suit, who wailed out the names Blue Demon and Cachorro Méndez. Upon hearing them, the wrestlers stomped out from behind the curtains. Two fleshy statues of testosterone, bulging out of their sparkly shorts and shiny tights, they thundered down the ramp, manes of hair spilling out from under their masks, and toward the ring, where they hoisted themselves in with one diagonal leap.

Once inside, the men lost no time in assaulting each other in whatever way they could. They grabbed each other's faces, yanked each other's hair, and tried to trip each other up in their gladiator boots, the taut cords of the ring constantly stretched and deformed as the quadrilateral changed shape each time a wrestler leaned into one side and catapulted himself back into the center. Tomás seemed completely gripped by the spectacle, in fact he was hardly aware of my presence, so I ignored him too, and we sat side by side watching two huge masses interlock as they came together and then shoved each other away, a constant attraction and repulsion, at moments reminding me of a bizarre hybrid that after merging its elements splits back into two, like bull and man melded into the formidable minotaur, who then, when separated again, find themselves in direct confrontation inside the ring.

I couldn't even tell for whom Tomás was rooting, for the *rudo* or the *técnico*, that is, for the man who played dirty or the man who played clean, but when Blue Demon was knocked down and unable to stand up despite the wave of hysteria and the dictionary of curses flung at him by the audience, Tomás stuck his fingers in his mouth and made a catcall that ricocheted off the roof and back into my ears. Blue Demon was hardly moving. A hush fell over the hall. The referee approached the collapsed pile of a man and with one theatrical tug he removed the blue-and-silver mask. And with that tug a baby face was revealed, and all strength and mystery extinguished.

During the next match, between El Espectro and Huracán Salgado, Tomás continued spellbound and in another or-bit, especially when El Espectro carried out a suicide dive, hurling himself headfirst out of the ring like a tormented rag doll (in a surprising act of generosity, his opponent caught the fall just in time). And I knew I stood no chance once the female wrestlers came on, La Reina Sombra and Felina Gutiérrez, pure muscle and curve in their leopard-print tights, tension coiled in their thighs as they trod down the ramp and swung themselves into the ring. From the front row three middle-aged women cried out for blood like those knitters at the guillotine, their faces contorted into storms as they bayed obscenities and punched the air.

On the way home Tomás, his battered station wagon ig-noring every red light, mentioned that the *luchas* were choreographed, the moves mostly planned out in advance. I said I was glad I hadn't known at the time, since it would've probably interfered with my enjoyment. But I wondered to myself about his display of suspense, why he had appeared so rapt when he'd known all along that the struggle wasn't real.

Despite the romantically arid night I felt drenched in testosterone, and once back in my room I couldn't shake off the sticky clammy atmosphere of the ring. The only antidote, I decided, drawing on available resources, that is, was to put on the Smiths; if anything were capable of neutralizing the virile concoction of Arena México, it would be them. I laid out the albums and dropped the needle onto "What She Said" and from there onto nine or ten other favorite songs. But I couldn't get the wrestlers out of my head, the wrestlers or Tomás, one seemed to highlight the other, the wrestlers so ardent, and Tomás so unlit; what would it take, I asked myself, to make this person come just a bit more alive. Sooner or later when listening to the Smiths I would have to think of my friend Patricio, who had Morrissey's autograph hanging on his wall, framed and behind glass. He'd been visiting London with his parents when he spotted Morrissey on the escalator of a famous department store, and quickly turned around and caught up with him. The singer was friendly, he said, in his blue jeans and striped polyester shirt, and signed the paper Patricio held out. We'd all pilgrimaged over to his house to study said autograph, it was far too valuable to leave the premises or even to be taken out of the frame, and both times I had gone I'd stared and stared at the childlike scrawl, in capitals, the tall *R*'s tilting forward as if going for a walk, and the curves of the *S*'s unfinished, like two upright parallel waves. But the curtain fell one drunken night when Patricio confessed he'd made up the story and forged the signature, though it was true he'd gone to London with his parents and this had been the outcome he'd been hoping for, and furthermore he'd practiced the signature so many times it really had begun to feel real. The main effect of listening to the Smiths was, obviously, a spike in longing, a longing for whatever one didn't have in life and perhaps never would, and as the needle danced over my loyal records I realized that more had to happen with Tomás, something had to be sealed, there had to be a sense of complicity; this was something I'd learned at the Burroughs apartment, complicity was what made two people a couple, regardless of how it all panned out.

I SOUGHT CALM WHILE THE OCEAN WAS RESTLESS,
the only hint of serenity the bluish gray of an indefinite
landscape in the distance, yet this ended up being nothing but more sea. At night its thunder was hard to bear,
and I'd have to remind myself how in the city silence was
also an impossibility, and that even on days when I didn't
leave home the city would force its way through the windowpanes. Our street wasn't busy but even so, the clamor
never ceased: car horns, the cries of ambulatory vendors,
deliverymen on motorcycles, radios playing on nearby
rooftops and patios.

From my hammock I tried to conjure up my favorite city
sound, that of the *tamalero* who'd announce dusk with his
disembodied cry. The cry grew louder as he drew nearer to

our home. He'd cycle past each evening, calling out *Ricos tamales oaxaqueños, compra tus tamales calientitos*, alerting everyone to the hot tamales in his cart. Sometimes when on the phone with a friend I would hear the same cry in the background and for a long while I thought the *tamalero* had the gift of ubiquity, until someone pointed out it was a recording activated by the turning of the bicycle pedals. The man's voice had apparently been recorded at his uncle's house when he was a teenager and had, like most city features, proliferated over time, eventually spreading to every corner, becoming the soundtrack to many people's evenings, not only mine. *Tamales oaxaqueños* belonged to no one, a mantra released at dusk like an orphaned balloon.

THE ELECTRIC BULB MAY HAVE BANISHED SHADOWS from the home but it enhanced all those beyond. The *fresas*, or rich kids, from school had their own haunts, places like El News, Bandasha, and Magic Circus (a megadisco with dance cages and light shows); I'd been to them a few times for birthdays and other celebrations, but for the most part I kept my distance, it was enough to see these individuals at school, why expose myself to them at night as well, to them and older versions of themselves, or the odd soap opera star from Televisa holding court over buckets of champagne. In fact, why head anywhere but to El Nueve, not even Tutti Frutti or Rockotitlán was as splendid, and whenever I was given permission to go out at night I nearly always went there.

El Nueve was the nocturnal reply to the daylight hours, the place that drew those of us who preferred European moonlight to the Mexican sun. Located halfway down Londres in the Zona Rosa, it played dark wave, post punk, and industrial, often courtesy of its Scottish DJ, an angular Goth who wore pointy boots and a black suede tassel jacket. At the entrance beckoned the sign ELLAS NO PAGAN, "women don't pay," and, even more alluringly, another sign, farther in: BARRA LIBRE, free drinks all night, although it was widely believed that ether was added to the ice to curb the drinking.

Nearly everyone was dolled up like a waxwork, powder-faced, ashen-faced, striking pose after pose. Some pulled it off while others exuded a stiff, stilted glamour. Tomás narrowed his eyes as I pointed out some of the regulars: there was Adán the Aviator, in his bomber jacket, goggles, motorcycle boots, and aviator cap with earflaps; he always seemed about to lift off yet in reality never left the dance floor. And standing against a wall wrapped in his melancholic aura was El Sauce Llorón, the weeping willow, a magazine editor by day and drama queen by night. Tall with a Roman nose, he was often in tears over insurmountable dramas, real and imagined, his long black hair framing his face like a shroud. It was known he had an on-and-off friendship with El Nueve's resident transvestites, Carlota and La Bogue, who presided over the rooms like exotic nocturnal flowers. And then there were Los Ultravox, a group of young men in beige raincoats, all in possession of deep voices and slicked-back hair.

It's like a permanent Day of the Dead in here, Tomás had complained, despite always being attired in black himself, and then added, on an entirely different note, And there's too much industrial, bring back the sovereignty of the guitar. At least he seemed appeased when the Scottish DJ put on the Stooges. One of Los Ultravox dropped to the floor and continued his dance there. Out of the corner of my eye I thought I glimpsed the leader of Los Anticristos, a gang with upside-down crucifixes tattooed on their temples who listened to the same music we did and every now and then turned up to jinx our nights by picking a fight, but thankfully the thin figure with a cane turned out to be a new bouncer. I drew Tomás's attention to the TV set suspended over the dance floor, which beamed specters from overseas. At that moment it was showing a video by the Human League, faces bathed in shadow and noir red lipstick. The speakers began barking out the industrial beats of Front 242. It was pretty funny, I said to Tomás a little timidly, how out of synch the images on the screen were from the melody in the club, indeed as out of synch as our inner picture often was from outer.

After our third round of vodka the TV screen went black and the fog machine was rolled out, followed by a clap of thunder and the choral surge of *Carmina Burana*. Signs of midnight. The dance floor was now officially open, and the fog machine released its plumes, which coiled around our legs like a dispatch from wintry lands, their glorious smell a metallic vanilla. Each week, the same theater, the same intoxication. La Bogue and two of Los Ultravox lit cigarettes. The smoke thickened and soon I could hardly see Tomás in front of me. Scared he would disappear or just melt into the ether, I grabbed on to his shirt, and once I had his shirt I leaned into the blankness and kissed him. It was as simple as that. Into the vanishing picture I reached out and showed, without having to show, what I wanted, and met no resistance. I could feel the gap between his teeth, not as distinctly as I'd imagined—I'd expected something nearly architectural—but there was no ignoring its presence, there like a gatekeeper at the front.

The smoke thinned as *Carmina Burana* segued into "Lucretia My Reflection." I shut my eyes and listened to the modulation. But my head began to spin and the floor drew away from me, as the ether, the dry ice, everything flooded in at once. One moment, I murmured to Tomás, and ran to the bathroom, where Doña Susana sat beside a tray of makeup and a plate of coins beside a mirror image of Doña Susana beside a tray of makeup and a plate of coins. I splashed water onto my face, as cold as it would get, and was patting myself dry with a paper towel when I spotted two cowboy boots emerging from under one of the stall doors, as if a person had collapsed.

I turned around and pulled the door open but there was no one. And yet I couldn't help sensing the presence of the girl who had overdosed in there one year ago, after swallowing an entire bottle of Valium. We'd found her just in time. She was on her own, as she always was, so our friend Paco had driven her to the hospital to have her stomach pumped. Her parents had arrived at two in the morning, freshly bathed, and her father had squeezed Paco's hand so tightly his bones nearly cracked. They stayed for ten minutes, whispered a few words to the doctors, and left. To the amazement of everyone, the girl had survived.

I hadn't thought about her for a while but now envisioned the scuffed boots from under the door, the black gummy bracelet tangled in her hair as we dragged her out, the denim jacket with a pack of filterless Camels stuffed into a pocket. I'd seen her many times, throwing her arms about the dance floor or fumbling in a corner with the Scottish DJ. In general she kept to herself, only entering into conversation to ask for cigarettes. Why was this person, this drama, from a year ago snaking its way into my thoughts? Tomás was in the other room and something was about to move forward, or perhaps just had, yet this scene felt more real than the one I'd extracted myself from and I felt too drunk and sick to return to the dance floor, so from the bathroom I cut across the bar area and rushed out onto the street, the ELLAS NO PAGAN sign a mockery since of course we *did* pay, payment was taken in other ways, and besides, by not paying one tends to owe even more.

I sat down on the steps of a closed chocolate shop to still my head and figure out what to do. There was a line at the taxi stand. It was too late to call my parents and ask them to pick me up. I could walk home, but recent reports of violence came wafting to mind. A few streets away the singer Jordi Espresso had been held at gunpoint for the kilo of gold hanging around his neck. He was fresh out of prison, where he'd spent years composing ballads about prison life, and therefore unarmed. Meanwhile, a rent boy had been stabbed on Hamburgo, and after staggering halfway down the block had collapsed on the hood of a Toyota parked outside the Duca d'Este café. In Polanco a girl and her bicycle were mugged on the corner of Dante and Tolstoi.

And then, a gift: my friend Mizfit, keys in hand, at his car. I'd been in his blue Golf many times, often up to eight of us piled on one another's laps, that's how romances often came about, heading to some distant party with conflicting addresses jotted down on scraps of paper, a caravan of cars, Mizfit usually leading the way, and he would get lost and the motorized caterpillar would follow, utter chaos and anticipation, the music on loud and windows rolled down, and in the end the party would take place in the car rather than at whatever intended destination. That night fortunately it was just me and Mizfit in his Golf, and I took deep breaths as he drove toward La Roma; the journey now seemed twice as long, and his car took every speed bump at the cruelest possible angle.

At Álvaro Obregón I asked to be let out. It was nearly one. Minimal signs of life troubled the streets. The odd car, relishing the freedom of empty space, hurtled past as I walked down the *camellón*, the wrought-iron benches vacant apart from the occasional tramp or infatuated couple. I tried to focus on my breathing—slowly, deeply—and avoided thoughts of Tomás and El Nueve. The vertigo was beginning to subside and yet I still felt full of ether.

I was about to turn off onto Orizaba when I noticed a strange scene lit by the streetlamps. Sometimes I saw the street kids from the Insurgentes roundabout splashing in the fountains, they'd leave their caps and shoes on the rim, but that night delivered a far more curious sight. A female figure, well past youth, in one of the fountains. She was cupping her hands and pouring water over her head, long tresses falling around her rather hunchbacked body, which in the wan light looked like an irregular pearl with misplaced curves and lumps. Her skin sagged in folds of varying thickness, and the rivulets added more creases as though she were bathing in a reverse fountain of youth. Had one of the fountain's Greek or Roman statues come to life, I wondered, or was my father having a laugh, was he, or was my vision, playing tricks on me, classical mythology acquiring a pulse, there on the streets of La Roma. But no, unlike the girl in the stall, she was present and real.

All of a sudden the figure turned in my direction and caught me staring. For a split second we locked eyes, and I realized she was the homeless woman who often sat outside the Sagrada Familia begging for alms on its steps, her skirt as petaled and billowy as the rose window overhead. They said she liked to nap in a pew in the final row, remaining comfortably until the caretaker would tap her on the shoulder to say they were closing the church for the evening. I'd also seen her sleeping on a bench, and at the 7-Eleven adding coffee to her cup of instant chicken soup. Despite her open-air address she was always remarkably clean, and I now saw why. Fearing I'd disturbed her, I quickly looked away and ran the last stretch to my house, my parents thankfully in bed by the time I let myself in.

NOW AT THE BEACH, I LOOKED BACK WITH NOSTALGIA on the cool, crepuscular grotto of El Nueve. Every shoreline should have at least one grotto, but Zipolite had none. It had bends and curves and some monumental boulders, maybe even a few concave places where one could hide, but it had no grotto to speak of.

If I hadn't seen the article, I can say for certain I would have never come to Oaxaca. If I hadn't happened to reach for yesterday's newspaper in the kitchen one afternoon, after shutting the windows and sitting down to my chili and avocado sandwich, the trip would have never taken place.

The television wasn't working so I'd turned to the only reading material at hand, yesterday's copy of *Excelsior*, and spread it out in front of me, allowing my eyes to wander from one crumpled page to the next as I took in the headlines—"Continual Theft in Cemeteries, Bones and Tombstones Missing"—"Dobermans and Tanks Evict Cardenistas"—"Price of Flowers Rises 500%, Authorities Remain Indifferent"—"Old Lady Found Seated in Armchair, Dead for Days"—"Suitcase Thief Detained at Airport." I was halfway through my sandwich when my eyes landed on a less familiar headline. Lurking on the outskirts of these stories was a different sort of news item, written in a different sort of voice:

"Ukrainian Dwarfs on the Run." Twelve Ukrainian dwarfs are on the run from a Soviet circus. The circus and the dwarfs had been touring Mexico since early October, both inland and along the coast. And then, without any warning, they were gone. According to authorities they vanished overnight with nothing but the costumes on their backs, green sequined suits with purple collars, and magenta shoes. After their performance in Xalapa, Veracruz, which, according to members of the audience, had been carried out with great poise and assurance, the troupe had returned to the rusty trailer in which they all slept, absenting themselves from dinner despite their notorious appetites, and in the morning when the German sword swallower knocked on their door, puzzled that not one of them had shown his

fɑce at breakfɑst or gone to help strike the tent, he was met with silence and, upon tentatively letting himself in, an empty trailer in disarray. After months of maltreatment at the hands of the ringmaster, the sword swallower surmised, the dwarfs had had enough. And so they took flight, with nothing but their costumes. No money, no passports, no language apart from their own, no letter or official seal to facilitate their passage. It was assumed by fellow performers, however, that they were on their way to the coast of Oaxaca.

Twelve Ukrainian dwarfs, escaped from a circus, on the loose, on the run, in our country. No more rules, no more authority. Flight! I tore the page out of the newspaper. I'd keep it in a drawer, no, in a book, no, in my bag. Always important to find a safe place for combustible material. I folded it eight times and slipped it in my bag, where it joined the usual jumble, and then finished, mechanically, the last bit of my sandwich, my thoughts now far removed from such a prosaic activity as eating. An idea was starting to form, an idea reinforced when I went for a stroll, sticking close to home since soon I'd have to return to tackle my homework, and as I walked I began to recall something my parents once told me, that our *colonia* was created in the early twentieth century by an Englishman named Walter Orrin whose family had founded the Circo Orrín, the first circus in Mexico to be powered by electricity, and he'd invested the profits in real estate

and even named the area La Roma in honor of the ancient Roman circus, and certain streets—Morelia, Orizaba, Tabasco, Veracruz—after places around the country
where his own circus had received the greatest applause.
A circus man built our neighborhood, Luisa, what do you
think of that?

I walked down those streets and down others, too, including Tonalá, where I stopped outside the Goethe
Institute to watch the students inside playing table football, enraptured by their game, and reflected on why it
was that most language centers had miniature football
tables, often placed near the window. I also paused outside our local pet store, and again through the window
I observed a cross-cultural communication of sorts, in
this case between a bright green parrot snatched from
the Lacandon Jungle and a cage-bred canary, and then
between a Persian cat, its face lost in a thicket of white,
and two skittish Siamese. How would the dwarfs fend for
themselves?

Perhaps we should call the newspaper and see whether
there's any further news, my mother said at dinner.
They too had seen the article.
I'm sure they'll appear, added my father. But now that you
mention vanishing acts, he said, turning to me, Basilia Lapadu called today. She says you haven't shown up for your
last three classes.

Mrs. Basilia Lapadu from Bucharest knew many languages and taught Italian at our school; even on the warmest of days, she wore woolen vests with rhomboid designs. She wasn't officially my teacher but that autumn my father had asked her to teach me Latin during my lunch break. At first it seemed like a good idea. My solitary lunches would now have a purpose. But before long, inattention and impatience took over. And Mrs. Lapadu was impatient too, constitutionally, and each lesson was an encounter between two short fuses, mine for having committed to learning Latin during my free time, and hers for having agreed to teach Latin during her free time to a girl who didn't fully acknowledge the sacrifice.

You committed to a semester.
I've changed my mind.
Later in life you'll be thankful. You will always have your Latin.

The article pitched up in my head but for a while remained dormant, the days driven by other distractions. One Sunday two men turned up with a long-necked truck and went along Álvaro Obregón snipping at the trees along the *camellón*, leaving some individuals looking miserably shorn. Our neighbor Yolanda from Chiapas opened a hair salon called Yolanda's of London where there'd once been a shop selling products from Michoacán. My mother's birthday: lunch out, a walk through Chapultepec Park, and, with diminishing attention, an evening at the theater. Another afternoon with Tomás at La Bella Italia, this time extensively sampling the jukebox despite a noticeable divergence in musical taste. And one day a new lock appeared on the door to the abandoned house, you could see it from a distance, it was so thick and shiny, along with a sign announcing the company Pérez y Morralla.

But the main development was the construction site. One Saturday morning I was woken up by the sound of a loud drill. I rose from bed and went downstairs just as my father was heading out to investigate. To our horror, we saw that the house next door was undergoing a transformation. It was barely 8:35 and already a dozen *albañiles* were engaged in various tasks, some taking a hammer to the wall, others a drill or a shovel to the ground, others erecting an immense scaffolding. From the looks of it, they were planning to gut the entire structure. A man in a linen suit was attaching a city permit to the vestiges of the gate.

Upon spotting him my father approached, identifying himself as the neighbor, and asked for an explanation. The man replied that the house, which had lain empty for years, had recently been purchased and that the new owners, a family from Monterrey, were planning many changes before they moved in. What sort of changes, my father inquired, and the man in the linen suit replied that the family had survived two kidnapping attempts and were moving to the capital in the hope it was safer than Monterrey but still wanted to fortify their house, so a security consultant, actually two, had advised them on what to build, what to tear down, what to install, what to enclose, basically how to convert their home into a fortress. And now that they'd been given the green light, the workers could begin. My father, clenching his fists, asked how many months the operation would take, to which the man replied, If we're lucky, no more than six. Six months, my father repeated, and the man said, Yes, well, if we're *very* lucky it will be closer to five, straining his vocal cords since at that moment the drill had started up again. And so it was that the empty house beside ours went from dormant ruin to anthill of activity, the inertia replaced by a babel of machines, the parched grass flattened by rubble, the rats and lizards no longer able to recognize their sanctuary.

From one day to the next, a whole new layer of noise was added to our street. The workers were usually arriving when I left for school, some sitting on the sidewalk eating their tortas, others beginning to set up. From time to time a monstrous cement mixer would spend the night outside, ready to resume its rotations in the morn. And one by one the banging and hammering and drilling would commence, one bang nearby, the next farther off, followed by a drilling so loud certain rooms in our house would vibrate. It sounded as though they were destroying rather than constructing, and every now and then there'd be an unrecognizable sound, somewhere between a bleat and a bellow, like a metallic animal in rage. Every movement, every sound, on our street was feeding, strengthening, empowering the construction site. When at home I was constantly aware of it, even in the evenings when the tools lay inert. And sometimes when I looked out my window one of the men would still be there hammering, a lone worker hammering at the dusk.

The *tamalero* began appearing earlier, in time for the workers to buy their tamales at the end of the day's labor. I would hear him asserting himself over the street as if his cart were carrying all the sounds it had crossed paths with, a great magnet that gathered city sounds like filings. The pre-recorded cry would move past our house till it merged with the construction noise, and one by one the voices of the tools and machines would leave off, first the hammers and then the drills and finally the cement mixer, and after a few minutes I'd look out and see eight or ten men crowding around the cart, eating their tamales.

My father had an office at the university but he did his writing from home, and the rectangular window in his study overlooked the construction site, providing him with a panoramic view of below. Goodbye to all those years of quiet, he said, as though the state of affairs were permanent, but he refused when my mother offered him her corner of the living room. He preferred to spend his hours staring down, tracking the workers' movements with such scrutiny the architect could have asked him for daily reports, and settled at his desk only when they took a break or went home in the evening. Years later, my father could still count on one hand the articles he'd written, and the chapter titles of the book he had attempted to write, against that mural of noise and activity.

On our corner in a grand colonial house lived an industrialist, one of the wealthy who stayed on after the earthquake, someone with a long name and a short CV. Whenever he was returning home he'd have his chauffeur klaxon his way down the street to announce his arrival, in time for the somber gates to slide open before he drove up. In every landscape there's an idiot who comes to destroy the silence, my father would say, and each time he said this I would think of the industrialist, although these days it wasn't quite silence he was destroying.

AND THEN ONE EVENING I FINALLY HAD THE CHANCE to air my idea, the idea that had begun to gather form as I walked the circus-named streets near home, an uneasy idea for sure, yet one I couldn't shake once it had gone somersaulting off in my head. There is no woodworm in the door hinges, someone once said, a good motto for any age, even at seventeen, and I knew it was wise to keep everything in motion.

BODYGUARDS REQUIRED TO PURCHASE TICKETS, read a sign in the foyer of the old cinema, but ours were invisible, and Tomás and I found seats, unshadowed, in a middle row.

Los Muñecos Infernales, The Curse of the Doll People, was a black-and-white film from 1961, with a relatively straight-forward plot. Four foolish archaeologists steal an idol from a voodoo temple in Haiti and bring it back to Mex-ico, where they soon face the consequences. The scenes cut between them and a cavern from where a witch doc-tor plots his revenge, sending out his murderous dolls to punish the men. The large dolls arrive in boxes, wrapped like children's toys, but once unwrapped they come alive to shed blood. It was hard not to cower as the little mur-derers advanced toward their victims holding long, poi-soned pins to plunge into their necks. And each time a doll murdered an archaeologist, it would acquire his face in the form of a mask. Yet I couldn't tell whether the actors behind these masks were children or small adults, and it was scarier not to know. The most thrilling moment was when a doctor conducted an autopsy on a doll that had been decapitated, running the scalpel down its tiny ster-num. As the walls of its chest began to cave in, the eyes in the head lying on the floor started to gleam, emanating such malice that several people around us gasped. Only then did Tomás and I grab hands, I can't remember who reached for whose, and by the time the film ended with a crucifix and a fire, the only two powers able to defeat the dolls and their voodoo, he had his arm wrapped tightly around my waist, and we continued in this clasp as we ex-ited the theater. My thoughts were focused on the points of contact and pressure to the exclusion of all other coordi-nates, and only minutes later did I realize he had led us to

La Casa de las Brujas, a café run by printers on Plaza Río de Janeiro, not far from the abandoned house. I live only a few streets away, I protested, let's go somewhere else, but he asked what I was hiding.

The interior was jovial despite the building's famously witchy façade. Each table had a paper cloth and a jar of crayons at its center. After we'd ordered beer and quesadillas, Tomás excused himself and said he was going to say a quick hello to his friend Matías, who worked in the kitchen. While he was gone I noticed an odd scene at the neighboring table. A man with an exuberant beard and creased flannel shirt with several missing buttons sat across from two girls, probably around ten and twelve, who greatly resembled him (as far as I could tell, beneath the foliage). They were very well dressed, in pink V-neck sweaters and pleated gray skirts and penny loafers— unlike the man, whom I had seen before, napping on a bench with a coat draped over his legs. He was now tearing at a loaf of white bread in a bag from Sumesa, stuffing chunks into his mouth as he spoke, while the girls hardly acknowledged his presence. Their eyes were fixed on the drawing they were making, a maze of loops and flourishes extending across the paper tablecloth.

This building, girls, he was saying in a fatherly tone, was designed by an architect named R. A. Pigeon. Because of course pigeons and architecture are impossible to untwine.

Did you hear what I just said, girls? Untwine. One of them glanced up at him, then at her sister, and resumed her drawing. Two glasses of a reddish juice, possibly watermelon, sat on the table alongside the loaf of white bread their father was now offering them, complemented by a block of supermarket cheese still in its plastic wrapping. He kept urging them to eat, tearing off more chunks of bread, laying them on the table, now opening the cheese with a butter knife, but the girls pretended they didn't know the man in front of them although I was quite certain it was their father. One pulled out a sparkly wallet, inside I could see several hundred-peso bills, and whispered something to her sister. They must live very comfortably with their mother and her new husband, I decided, and once a month were obliged to meet up with their father, who was estranged and lost to the streets, and sometimes when they had an appointment he would fail to show up. Yes, this was the story, I thought to myself as the man gorged on bread and cheese. I suspected he had a few conspiracy theories swirling around his head, ideas he may have wanted to share, but the girls' minds were on other matters, among them the nice warm dinner waiting at home. They weren't even allowed to order anything on the menu apart from juice; nothing of interest, apart from the jar of colored crayons.

Stop staring, it's rude. Tomás had returned to our table and was watching me, all of a sudden concerned with etiquette. I asked whether he'd found his friend. Yes, he had . . . and launched into a half-funny, half-tedious monologue about how his friend preferred the hot chocolate in the last café where he'd worked, there it was thick and full of spices, but here they followed a different hot chocolate philosophy, and . . . We had just been to the movies, had sat side by side in darkness, and were both now already distracted by other people. The waiter brought us our food just as the man and his daughters stood up to leave, the father tucking a stack of napkins into his bag, and hurried out, the girls one step ahead, as if they'd realized they were running late.

What was that all about? Tomás asked. I explained my theory about the separate lives being led by the father and his daughters, the man on the street and the girls in luxury. He said he would rather be in the man's shoes, completely free, and I couldn't help agreeing with him. After we'd finished eating we each plucked a crayon, red and green, from the jar. Tomás drew my face, I drew his, neither of us a born artist by the looks of it, but soon we'd filled up more than half the tablecloth with our sketches.

So, what else have you been up to apart from school, Goths, and shipwrecks, he asked, what keeps you busy the rest of the time? I mentally ran through the images of my life; nothing seemed exciting enough to mention, until it occurred to me to tell him about the dwarfs. I'd been meaning to, and there in La Casa de las Brujas, as we sat fending off awkward pauses with the crayons in our hands, seemed like an ideal moment. Unable to recall the details, I invented a few along the way—*some dwarfs excelled at the tightrope, others at the trapeze; in their trailer they found overturned powder jars, ribbons cascading from the sink, and a half-eaten apple; the acrobat from Tbilisi was heartbroken, she had been engaged to the most handsome dwarf, never without his pipe, and they'd been planning to have many children.* I watched with satisfaction as Tomás leaned forward in his seat, it was magnificent to command all his attention, and I tried to come up with more details but before I could throw in another handful he interrupted.

So where are they now?
The circus people say they ran off to Oaxaca.
Oaxaca?
Yes, somewhere along the coast.

He reached for the blue crayon and began to draw a coastline, his hand wandering this way and that until it trailed off at the table's edge.

I love Oaxaca.
You do?
Especially Zipolite.

He added stick figures, trees, and a hut.

Zi-po-li-te, I repeated, adding that it sounded like an incantation.

Yes, lots of towns in Oaxaca sound like excerpts from magic spells. Juchitán, Tlacolula, Yalalag, Yanhuitlán . . .

The blue crayon spelled them out.

When were you last there?
Last year. Autumn's the best time to go.

I tried to build on that but the words caught in my throat. He added tall waves to the drawing.

Yeah, autumn's the best time. There are still tourists but not as many. At the beach, anyway.

And then I aired the idea that had, until that instant, only been an idea, dipping in and out of other thoughts, destined to perhaps remain nothing more:

Why don't we go? Let's go to Oaxaca and find the dwarfs.

Tomás stared at me, wide-eyed, and drank from his beer.

Are you serious?
Yes, let's go.

A brief silence.

But will your parents let you? Don't you have school?

I listened to myself speak.

Well, yes . . . I do have school but it's probably okay if I miss a few days. And I probably shouldn't tell my parents since I'm not sure they'd give me permission.

Tomás studied my face without speaking, the crayon motionless in his hand. I couldn't tell whether he was shocked, impressed, or both.

Okay, Luisa, let's do it.

We can start at the top of the coast and work our way down.

Let's start in Zipolite.

But it doesn't make sense to start in the middle of the coast.

We can start anywhere we like.

I wanted to throw in a caveat, some sort of clause, but none came to mind.

Don't worry, you'll love Zipolite. And if they know anything about anything, your dwarfs will be there.

Zi-po-li-te. Mouthing the four syllables, I finished off what was left of my beer and smiled uncertainly at the map he had drawn, its tall waves and trees and stick figures, an unfinished sketch of the place we might occupy. Before leaving La Casa de las Brujas I tore off the section of the paper with the landscape and rolled it up, and once home I hid it behind a coat in my closet, just in case someone might be able to identify the exact bend of the coastline.

ZIPOLITE HAD AN ASTRONOMY THAT BLAZED ACROSS
the night sky but by morning it would dissolve into con-
stellations of somnambulist men and women traipsing
across the sand, some of them aware, possibly, that in
Spanish *resaca* means both hangover and undertow. As I
roamed the beach I thought back on my favorite sign on
the Periférico, which featured enormous neon math instruments made by BACO. It had been there since I was a
child, the instruments all acting out their functions with
their rotating arms, the scissors opening and closing, the
compass going around and around, the ruler, the lead
pencil, each measuring the lengths and widths of days, directions taken and not taken. In Oaxaca I was beyond the
perimeter, far beyond, I could take whatever route, choose
whatever distance.

Each time I'd passed the BACO sign hovering over the streams of cars, measuring something greater than the traffic, I'd felt invigorated, and certain of my decision. Yet the days leading up to the trip were haunted by loud daydream and silent debate, by second thoughts and moments of panic. For the most part, however, daydream defied guilt, a guilt toward my parents that at times grew to colossal proportions, especially over dinner, hanging over the table like a clunky chandelier, but once I'd returned to my room it would shrink back to something more tolerable.

At times I thought of the distress it would unleash on them, and at times it made me sick, yet never sick enough to call off the trip. Well, more than a trip it felt like a fugue, a melody consisting of opposing elements that interweave, two independent tunes that eventually join up and once merged turn into fugitives, fugitive notes that escape through the bars of their musical stave. I was seventeen, and the time had come to assert my independence—look at Tomás, who had left home and gone to live with an uncle, and Julián, who lived in unusual circumstances of his own design; for long enough I'd accepted life just as it was, and before Oaxaca I worked harder than ever, completing my homework hours before bedtime, and listened attentively to my father's impromptu lectures. Open doors, reminders of all those days you could have left your room and didn't. And of the times you did leave and wish you hadn't. Open doors kill the promise of focus and finality, never trust anything that can change angle so cleanly.

Little did my father know that whatever he spoke about now seemed relevant to the plan, whether it strengthened my resolve or fed my indecision. And yet it remained the case that ships on the ocean floor were far more interesting than those on its surface, and I couldn't help peering into the books in his study that contained turquoise-green photographs depicting ghostly masses lying aslant on the seabed, great silhouettes once propelled by wind, then by water.

At dinner he continued to speak of stormy seas and overloaded boats, of cargo being taken places against its will. In the Antikythera shipwreck, for instance, there was one lost horse, a great marble statue that proved too difficult to heave out, and it tumbled back into the depths, choosing the sea, and was there to this day, the horse that gave them the slip, galloping along endless banks of seabed, kicking up whole paragraphs of sand.

Every shipwreck was a story sealed and unsealed, my father would say, and vulnerable to modern intrusion. Intrusion by looters and prospectors and amateur marine archaeologists, but also intrusion by the octopus, a well-known scrambler who rummages through wrecks in search of objects with which to furnish its garden, and in its pursuits it contaminates, or scrambles, the information. It too can ruin the chronological harmony.

Chronological harmony.

Accounts of the octopus lightened matters. Whereas any mention of the sponge divers of Symi tended to darken the picture. The men dived vertically, twenty meters down, holding their breath as they cut free as many sponges as they could from the seabed. Even if I'd been a good swimmer I would have found the image unsettling, and the thought of the pressure on their lungs as they scavenged till the last possible moment and then rushed back up for air, and upon returning to the surface often succumbed to narcosis or the bends, reminded me, as if one needed reminding, of our dramatic contract with the ocean.

ON ONE AFTERNOON OF PARTICULAR INDECISION when even the map in the closet didn't have the power to sway, a torrential rain began to fall. It was the sort of rain that hardened into hail, and the kind of storm that killed the electricity for hours. Sometimes our Mexican tempests were truly biblical. Our last big storm had claimed the lives of nearly sixty horses at an equestrian club in Tecamachalco. Trapped in their stables and unable to escape the three-meter deluge, most had drowned and the rest were dragged away by currents of mud and water. We'd seen it on the news. Their elderly keeper had tried to free them but died in the attempt, later found buried under a mausoleum of bricks. They showed footage of the horses' limp bodies being hauled out by pickup trucks, their heads dangling and coats caked in mud, while jockeys and families gazed tearfully from the sidelines. That had been the last intense storm and then came this one, one afternoon in late October; the rainy season had ended but something took hold of the sky.

I'd been home from school for over an hour. My father was still at the university, my mother out giving a translation workshop. A steady rain drummed at the windows as I stretched out on the sofa in the living room. From where I lay, my head propped up by two pillows, I could see the piano inherited from my grandparents, with the same musical score gathering dust for as long as I could remember, it was all my mother wanted to play, this "Rage Over a Lost Penny" by Beethoven, in fact I associated it so much with this piano I would have been startled had anything else emerged from its innards. And there draped over the piano stool, my father's olive-green jacket, the grooves of the corduroy too eroded to still be distinct; it was his favorite jacket and he wore it far more often than my mother played the Beethoven, yet that day he'd left home in something else.

The trip. My parents. The trip. My mind leapt between one and the other, and there was no way to reconcile them. I began to wonder whether I should call it off, explain to Tomás that I needed to remain in the city for college interviews; I was trying to think toward some near-distant future, in fact more near than distant, and was applying to universities abroad. Any day there might be a professor visiting from Europe or the United States who would be summoning me at short notice for an interview. Yes, that's what I would tell him, that I couldn't go to the beach but still wanted to see him as much as possible in the city. I had to remain there, on standby.

The rain built in sound and volume, then turned into hail, and from one instant to the next every light was struck, every electrical current severed. I lit three candles, wicks twitching as the walls trembled with each peal of thunder. A giant hand of wind grabbed our house and rattled it. One of the candles went out. I heard sounds from other rooms, the opening and closing of boxes, objects in my father's study starting to multiply. I didn't want to be alone for a second longer. I threw on my coat and rushed out onto the street, into a punctuation mania of the elements, the angry question marks of car horns—traffic lights on the blink—and the exclamation marks of antisocial rain beating down on heads and shoulders, and ran from awning to awning till I reached the Covadonga, soaked by the time I arrived.

I found a lighter in my bag and groped my way upstairs, glimpsing undefined figures on every floor and the firefly tips of people's cigarettes. And, at the top, Julián, installed at a fold-out table accompanied by two candles. He stood when he saw me, as if expecting a visitor, footsteps

always louder in the dark, and led me to where he sat. Our
voices lowered and then rose as the rain lashed the metal
door that gave onto the balcony. A drip announced a leak
nearby. Julián repositioned the candles in such a way that
new shadows were born on the wall behind us. Obeying
a sudden command from within, I said to him, Show me
some goblins. He held up a hand and tried unsuccessfully
to cast a monster. No . . . He clasped his hands together
again and this time produced a wolf, which of course was
not a monster, I complained, so he had another go and
finally created a pointy-eared being that was obligingly
more goblinesque, and after that a snaggle-toothed creature, equally menacing, and then it was my turn, and I
pressed my hands together and raised and lowered them
in such a way as to create what looked like a fantasy com-
posite swooping through the air or plowing through the
waves in search of prey.

After a few minutes of admiring the menagerie, though I
wished we'd given each a slightly longer lifespan, Julián
pushed the candle as its light chased the shadows chased
the wolf, and we sat without speaking, listening to the rain.
The first candle neared its end, soon to leave us with only
one. As it sputtered out in a final smoky wisp, he drew
my face to his and kissed me, a tender kiss, more fraternal
than erotic, after all, he liked Carlota the trannie and I
liked Tomás, and for several minutes we kissed, there in
near darkness save for one timid candle, nothing touch-

ing but our mouths. Once the rain began to subside Julián walked me downstairs illuminating the way, and I stepped out into the wet murky streets. Most features around me, from the uninhabited sidewalk to the slumbering shops and streetlamps, felt like shadow play and illusion, and once again I felt lifted by new, wild thoughts. By the time I reached my house, my parents waiting with long faces—I hadn't left a note—I was certain I would go to Oaxaca.

A SUNDAY LIKE A CLOSED DOOR. MONDAY, A DOOR
forced open.

The morning of our trip arrived, the time to grant further
dimension to the drawing. I was relieved the countdown
had ended. It was still dark when I awoke to the sound of
the newspaperman tossing the paper over the gate, the
thud as it hit the damp ground and the fading zoom of
his motorcycle. Once dressed I paused in the doorway of
my room to cast a final glance around, but nothing held
me back, no door, no object, no angle. I had packed my
bag the night before—a sun hat; red lipstick; two T-shirts,
a little dress, and a wraparound skirt; my black bikini;
a pair of sandals; a miniature sample of Obsession; the
Penguin paperback of Lautréamont's *Chants de Maldoror*

that Mr. Berg had lent me; my Walkman and, after great deliberation, a selection of tapes (Depeche Mode's *Speak and Spell*, Joy Division's *Unknown Pleasures*, Siouxsie and the Banshees' *Tinderbox*, the Jesus and Mary Chain's *Barbed Wire Kisses*, the Cure's *Three Imaginary Boys*, and Nick Cave and the Bad Seeds' *Tender Prey*); and a purse with money, 200 pesos in total, my escapade financed by a handful of friends who'd given donations ranging from ten to twenty. Satisfaction: my fugitive bag fit into my capacious obedient one, meaning I'd raise no suspicions when I left for school.

I saw my mother only briefly, our paths crossing in the kitchen. Flustered by an unpaid bill she'd found lying on the counter, her only preoccupation apart from numbers—she didn't notice I was hardly eating—was whether to have tea or coffee. It was a similar crisis each morning, the mouse of indecision running between the two, but after a few seconds she would always choose coffee. That morning, however, she seemed truly unable to decide, and put on the kettle before also switching on the coffee machine. Indecision accompanied her in most tasks, a habit, if it could be regarded as that, she'd acquired while translating; she would sit for hours at her desk or the piano top caught between words, succumbing to the force field of one and then another, and when I saw her so immobilized I couldn't help thinking she should've been a tightrope walker instead, that was the ideal profession for the indecisive, with only one path to take, forward, the distance determined before you even set out; you cannot take a left or right or a sudden diagonal, your journey is simply from A to B or from B to A, and all you control is the speed. That morning I had no room for indecision, there's always a danger it's contagious, and was relieved when she switched off the kettle and turned her full attention to the coffee machine. Yawning as she tightened the belt on her robe, still in a fog she asked what I wanted for lunch later that day. I looked away guiltily and mumbled the name of a favorite soup.

The machines of the construction site lay asleep but in the plaza the old organ grinder sat by the fountain polishing his instrument. The sun painted the tops of trees and the uppermost corners of windows. The wind flipped through the pages of an abandoned magazine. I hurried past a cluster of shops selling hearing aids, imagining the gadgets inside amplifying my steps, and once on the bus chose a seat by the window and laid my bag beside me so no one would join. That morning the Swedes played Yazoo. I tried to concentrate on the singer's hefty voice, in dialogue with the keyboard whose tunes alternated between happy and forlorn, and allowed my nerves to be buffeted between the two. But just as the bus was crossing Chapultepec Park's *tercera sección*, the music stopped. Someone cursed, first in Swedish and then in English. Their batteries had run out.

The only other time the stereo had gone quiet was on the morning of the earthquake. As we'd crossed the city in apocalyptic collapse, the driver braking every now and then as he tried to decide whether to complete the journey or bring us home, the Swedes, once they realized the scale of the horror, had switched off their music. When we reached the school gates a policeman told us to turn around, classes would be suspended until further notice, and the driver returned us to our homes one by one. This was the last time, as far as I knew, we'd had total silence on the bus, a requiem without notes or music or ascension.

That Thursday at the end of classes instead of the school bus I boarded a Ruta 100 and went to meet Tomás at TAPO, one of the city's four bus terminals, each corresponding to a cardinal point, in this case Oriente. To some the terminal may have seemed like a kaleidoscope of shifting landscapes, beams of light that changed color and pattern with every rotation, but to less foreign eyes like ours it was a cauldron of bad moods and coyotes on the prowl, its noisy hall full of bewildered tourists, pirate taxi drivers, and street vendors all jostling for space. From every corner, bus companies—Estrella Blanca, Cristóbal Colón, and Oaxaca Pacífico—competed for passengers. By the time we returned from the taquería across the street it was nearing five, at least according to the large clock that watched over the terminal with a skeptical eye, but the afternoon heat, trapped in the limbo of imminent departures, told a different hour, and we sat on our bags, restless and cranky, as more and more vendors arrived balancing racks of food on their shoulders or dragging sackfuls of trinkets they would decant onto a polyester blanket.

Finally Tomás, who held our tickets, signaled it was time to board. In the terminal's hinterland our Oaxaca Pacífico bus was waiting, shuddering as it warmed its joints for the long journey ahead. Dozens of eyes tracked our movements as we shuffled down the aisle, our fellow passengers mostly men from the countryside, some with their wives, the overhead racks sagging and bulging with parcels. Our assigned seats were in the middle, across from two elderly men who studied Tomás as he lifted our bags onto the rack. It was an old bus, probably from the seventies, with faded pink-and-blue-checked seats and entire maps scratched into the windowpanes. I asked to sit by the window; Tomás was familiar with the route but I'd traveled to Oaxaca only by plane, with my parents. Once seated I leaned back and grabbed his cool hand as the driver tore through the city, tore through its outskirts, and tore down the first stretch of highway before relaxing into a more leisurely speed.

Dusk blurred the features of the landscape, the outlines of billboards and the spectral needles of telephone poles

growing scanter the farther we got from the city. Tomás
and I plugged into our Walkmans, the Specials for him
and Nick Cave for me, while the engine purred beneath
my seat, and for a few blissful hours I felt we were moving
through a universe in which space and matter were orga-
nized in just the right way. After Nick Cave I put on Joy
Division. As much as I loved *Unknown Pleasures*, I began
to wish I'd brought their other album, *Closer*. *Unknown
Pleasures* had "New Dawn Fades" and "She's Lost Control,"
but *Closer* had "Decades," "Isolation," "Passover," and "A
Means to an End." In other words, it had more songs that
meant something to me. A hopelessly tiny predicament, I
tried telling myself, I wasn't going to be away forever and
once at the beach I'd probably have no need for music. But
I kept thinking of the songs I didn't have rather than the
ones I'd brought along.

We had just turned a dangerous curve when my Walkman
batteries ran out. By then I'd moved on to Depeche Mode.
With little warning, the voice and the synths began to slur
as if mired in reams of magnetic tape. I shook my miniature stereo, removed the batteries, reinserted them in an
alternative order. To no avail. I glanced at Tomás. As far as
I could tell, he hadn't run into a similar problem. I made
a sign for him to remove his headphones. No more battery, I said, no more music. How many hours left? Quite a
few, he replied, *but don't worry*, and extracted a white pill
from his pocket, some kind of -zepam he'd purchased at

the pharmacy, diazepam or lorazepam or clonazepam, as easy to buy as aspirin, he said, and suggested I start with half. I washed it down with some warm Sidral and waited for it to dissolve in my system.

Gradually the armrest, the window, the figures around me lost their focus, and I recalled a book someone once brought to school containing photographs of spiderwebs woven after the spiders had been given different drugs (peak activity of web construction being around four in the morning). The scientists had delicately removed the spiders and sprayed their webs white, then photographed these against a black background, the resulting images like negatives that revealed the darkroom, the industry, of night. I tried to recall some of the patterns. Caffeine was the greatest disrupter, producing highly irregular spacing and very big gaps between the radii. LSD inspired webs whose threads spread widely outward like the rays of the sun. As for diazepam or whatever sedative they administered in drops of sugary water, at that moment I couldn't remember what patterns had emerged, only that the spider's activity levels had been greatly reduced. But how convenient to go through life with silk as your currency, and all movement from the periphery inward.

With this in mind I sank farther into my seat as the bus penetrated the landscape, a landscape that held what felt like equal amounts of promise and danger, the thought

stirring enough to keep me wakeful despite my wonder-
fully drowsy state, and in this state I observed from the
window the ragged cacti and hilltops, assertive verticals
on an inert plane, and every now and then the sad sight of
a run-over dog, its carcass spotlit for a few seconds by the
headlights.

Tomás was fast asleep by the time our bus began to skim
the fragile rims of ravines, past the tops of tall, ancient
trees, a heart-bursting drop just feet away from where we
sat. I grabbed his hand but it was limp so I borrowed his
Walkman instead. It still had some battery, and I listened
to the Specials until there, too, the voices slowed down and
then ceased completely. And once that was gone I reached
into his pocket—he didn't react—and found the second
half of the pill. We still had hours to go and I didn't want
to be the only person awake, everyone around me now
asleep apart from the driver. I could see the back of his
head and if I strained my eyes the top half of his face in the
rearview mirror, though before long he switched off the
light, plunging us into a kind of oblivion, the only sounds
of life the engine's steady pulse and a cumbia playing softly
on the radio.

The landscape began to feel compressed, features that usually lived far apart now uneasily close, *cloudsroadsmoun-
taintops*, and I had eased into almost total tranquillity
when all of a sudden the bus came to a halt. Lights on.

Driver's voice down the aisle. A drug search: all women
off. Along with eight others I stepped out into the shiv-
ering night, exposed to the spirits and highway bandits
known to populate the caves by the roadside, but the pill
kept me calm as I stood looking up into the windows of
the bus. Four policemen were shining their torches into
each man's face, including the pale moon of Tomás's, and
patting their pockets, an operation that fortunately did
not last long since they found nothing but a few pills and
cigarettes, and after ten minutes they disembarked and
sped off on their sputtering motorcycles, allowing our bus
to recommence its journey to the coast.

It was deep night when we arrived in Zipolite. One by one
we stepped off and dispersed. I held on to Tomás's arm
as the sand gave way beneath our feet, the warm salty
air exuding its welcome as the ocean roared territorially
nearby, and we walked in a direction that could have been
left or right or straight ahead. The dim form of a woman
appeared and from this form emerged a voice that offered
an open-air palapa for ten pesos a night or a bungalow
with walls for twenty. She switched on her flashlight to il-
lustrate the first option: a thatched structure held aloft by
four poles, containing two hammocks side by side. We'll
take it, we said in unison. Exhausted from our travels despite having slept on the bus, we remained in our clothes

and deposited our shoes on the sand below. By the time the overhead lamp reached the end of its wick Tomás had drifted off and soon I too was able to hand myself over to sleep, despite a loud whirring of wings followed by an abrupt silence, as if a large insect had come to land on the cords of my hammock.

FOR AS LONG AS I COULD REMEMBER—SOME POINT IN early childhood when I began to distinguish one landscape from another—beaches had had an unsettling effect on me. I did not love the water particularly, nor the heat, nor was I given to long spells of repose. Other shorelines didn't trouble me. Only the beach. And yet here I was. I had no desire to speak as we tipped out of our hammocks and onto the hot sand that first morning, clusters of palm trees waving like hunched trolls in the wind. Behind us lay hills and fields of corn and before us the waves of the Pacific, rolling and peaking and breaking. Resisting the urge to explore, we decided first on breakfast—we hadn't eaten since leaving the city—and after putting on my hat and sunglasses I followed Tomás along the shore to his favorite *fonda*, El Cósmico, the name, hand painted in pink

letters on a splintering board, at odds with its humble di-
mensions: three sloping tables, their legs half sunken in
the sand, and six subservient chairs.

A young girl in a red strapless dress recited the dishes of the
day—fish in mango sauce, fish in mole poblano, breaded
fish with something or other. I asked whether there was
any dish without fish. The girl looked at me curiously and
fetched her mother, a more weathered version of herself,
in a matching red dress. The woman offered to make me
tacos de calabacita for five pesos more. Yes, please, I said
quickly. We need to keep an eye on the money, Tomás
muttered once the woman had walked off. I reminded
him that I was a vegetarian, a fact he knew, but still he
rolled his eyes in the irksome way that carnivores often
had. I didn't think fish counted, he added, which made me
further recoil, yet I mumbled a reply, Nothing that lives,
which was indeed a pact I'd made with the animal kingdom on the day I turned fourteen. You'll stop growing,
my parents had protested, but once I'd listened to "Meat Is
Murder" and the decision had been made I knew I would
never go back. How to justify a life extinguished for the
fleeting pleasure of a meal, a meal forgotten as soon as the
next one came along? There were few matters about which
I felt as strongly, yet most of the time I kept my thoughts
to myself, and on that first morning, across from Tomás at
the blue table with its legs half sunken in the sand and the
ocean beckoning meters away, I reined in my irritation.

There I was, sitting with Tomás Román, beneath an insistent sun that didn't let us forget its presence. He had traded his fitted black garments for linen, white and baggy, and there was something cloudlike about his appearance, vague and undefined, that didn't suit him. But this was TR, I told myself, TR. The same person from the *luchas*, the cinema, the abandoned house, the person whose name adorned my notebooks. But even his expression had changed, it wasn't as playful or maverick as it had seemed at first. Perhaps all would become clearer at sea level, free from the giddiness created by the city's high altitude. Yes, now that I considered it, most actions in the city were probably carried out in a state of semi-giddiness, surely living at 2,250 meters above sea level impaired one's judgment, and we all suffered from a strain of mountain sickness without being in the mountains.

Now at point zero, it was possible the picture would come into focus, as it did when I happened to mention how kind it was of him to give the organ grinder a coin that morning. I had witnessed the event, I told him, while on my way to school, to which Tomás shrugged and said it had been an old one-peso coin, no longer in circulation, which he'd been carrying around in his pocket and wanted to get rid of. The organ grinder probably hadn't noticed, at least not immediately, he was old and his eyes were full of cataracts, though he might have tried using it later that day to buy his lunch and the person in the shop would have returned it to him . . . I winced at his words, half wishing I hadn't heard them, but it was too late, and in an effort to control the anger that was quietly on the rise I shook off my sandals and sank my feet into the sand and felt nearly as cheated as the man.

The girl in the red dress returned with our food, accompanied by three sauces and two bottles of beer. I wasn't certain they'd been part of our order but by then they were welcome. Shortly afterward her mother materialized to ask whether we needed anything further. No, we said, but she hovered, keen to enter into conversation. One could tell she was used to chatting with her customers. Expected it. Resting her hands on the back of my chair, the woman asked where we were from. Mexico City. And were we good swimmers? Yes, Tomás said. I didn't reply. Had we been to Zipolite before? Many times, he said, with a hint of impatience. And what did we think of what was happening in the country, the presidential election and the recount and the machines and the rest? As she spoke her longest sentence she came to stand in front of us; I noticed a rather prominent gold tooth in her mouth, second on the left and larger than the others. Tomás mumbled a few words about corruption, that it was everywhere so what could you expect, and reached for his beer.

Once the woman had delivered her questions she provided us with some local lore. After telling us about the famous people who had come through Zipolite, mainly the Rolling Stones, though she couldn't remember whether all four had come or possibly two or maybe only the singer, she mentioned a recent incident, in fact people were still talking about it and it had happened right here on the beach, right here in front of El Cósmico, right here in Zipolite. Four Zapotec girls from a neighboring village had decided to go into the water despite none of them knowing how to swim; despite their usual modesty these girls had removed their clothes and run into the waves laughing and crying out in a language no tourist could understand, they'd taken off their bracelets and their earrings and laid them on the sand beside some trinkets they'd been selling—peculiar circumstances, it was agreed, for which there was no accounting—yet no one took much notice until their bodies washed ashore, one by one, and then there was panic, only then, and someone ran to fetch the lifeguard, but by the time the lifeguard appeared the ocean had entered everywhere.

Now, what do you think of that? the woman asked. I laid down my fork and shook my head, uncertain of what to say. Tomás picked up a toothpick and began chewing on it, his face twisting up each time he bit down, as if concerned the story might ruin his meal. So, what do you think? the woman asked a second time. Terrible, I said insufficiently. And then, sensing a pause, though it wasn't quite the right moment, I asked whether she had seen any dwarfs. No, she frowned, she hadn't. Her daughter called out from another table. More guests had arrived. Once she'd left, taking her story with her, Tomás explained that this *fonda* was named El Cósmico because Zipolite was the center of the cosmos, or at the very least one of its centers, it had better vibes than any other beach he'd ever been to, and that's because you could toss your baggage into the ocean and knowledge from the cosmos would wash back ashore. How could there be more than one center, I felt like asking, plus isn't the cosmos meant to be merciful and these girls had just drowned, but he was speaking loudly and excitedly and I didn't have the energy to raise my voice to interrupt. If there was one thing I had an aversion to, I thought to myself as Tomás took a bite of fish and carried on speaking with his mouth full, it was this use of the word *cosmos*, in my mind *cosmos* had to do with Soviet cosmonauts rather than seaside philosophy. Zipolite was part of any metaphysical map, Tomás continued. Well, who drew these maps, I felt like asking, but let him ramble on. Any metaphysical map would include this beach, he rephrased, it's an important slice of the universe, right here where we're sitting. He started to list the reasons, among them a certain movement of the ocean and reception of the sand, and moreover, Zipolite was one of the few nudist beaches in Mexico, he informed me since I had yet to see for myself, though nudity was optional. As he spoke I studied him through my sunglasses, his white baggy top denting in the breeze, and asked myself again whether this was the same person from the streets of La Roma. Half an hour later the girl returned with a slip of paper on which was written 26 PESOS, bringing our first cosmic visit to an end.

A STRIP OF SAND, A CLUSTER OF TREES, A BAND OF waves, a band of sky: the beach looked like a naïve composition, the stock motifs laid out, ready for a pair of scissors to come and create a gap, a boundary, where there failed to be one, to separate water from sky. Yet there were a few objects that disturbed the horizon, such as a blue hut on wheels that seemed to change location depending on the tide. Primitive and compact, it perched near some boulders, somehow in disagreement with the mood of the beach, the sort of dwelling one might expect to find in the depths of a forest rather than on the coast. At moments I simply sat and stared at the hut, waiting for it to speak.

• • •

It was day three, or four, and the light wind that nipped at the shore soon dropped to a mild breeze. Most people were wading in the water or sprawled out like freakish crabs at its edge. Even as a child, I would notice how silly beach-goers always looked, lolling on their backs or losing their poise as they tried to advance in the sand, and all those adults who dozed off like possums and woke up burned into varying shades of red.

Every now and then I'd catch Tomás watching me in silence.
What are you thinking?
Nothing, he'd say, and turn away.

And then, moments later:

And what, exactly, will we do once we find these dwarfs of yours?
They're not mine.
What will we do when we find them?
Let's find them first and then see.

It was after one of these exchanges that he pointed to a cluster of palms and said, I'll race you to those trees. I wondered for a moment why he had suggested it. In order to alleviate the silences, I assumed, or to appease a mounting agitation. Despite weekend cigarettes I was one of the fastest runners at school, even faster than most boys, and I sensed I'd outrun him. But I was quite comfortable where I sat, was beginning to embrace the lethargy, and didn't feel like moving. I heard myself say yes. No sooner had the word left my mouth than Tomás shot off full speed, and I right after. I saw him in my peripheral vision. There he was in front of me. Alongside. Somewhere behind. A moment of elation—before I sensed I was running alone. I slowed down to check by how much I had outstripped him and saw, to my total surprise, Tomás running in the opposite direction. Entirely, diametrically, opposite. He was shrinking in size, soon impossible to distinguish from the other dots around him. For a few moments my heart did a little jump but soon returned to its place, and I looked around to see whether anyone had witnessed what had just occurred: a boy running from a girl, off and away in a burst of white.

I retraced my steps to the spot from where we'd set off and tried to understand what had just happened. Tomás had proposed a game of sorts and then used it to run in the other direction. The tears and creases in the picture, had he been seeing them too? Or perhaps he was preempting me, rushing to become the one who broke things off, words smothered like a nascent fire, one of countless *I think it's best if* . . . guillotined by pride. Theory three: he had caught sight of someone he knew, or realized he'd forgotten something, and hurried off to that person or thing. No, it was almost certainly theory number one or two.

I went over moments in the city and their particulars. The fact, for instance, he'd simply walked past the émigrés and their ancient dog—surely a more gallant individual would've had the impulse to stop and offer his assistance? And his macabre stare in the Burroughs flat. And the disconnect at the *luchas* and the cinema, a poor match I was for the wrestlers and murderous dolls. Not to mention the latest revelation of the organ grinder's coin.

Unable to settle the question in my head, I swapped my growing confusion for hunger, theoretically easier to address, and inquired at two *fondas*. Both offered the usual quesadilla, nothing more, and I couldn't handle another slab of cheese and tortilla. Beyond a cluster of rocks I finally came upon a fruit seller with a green apron that came down to his knees. He'd set up a tiny stand and was busy cleaving his fruit in half with a machete, first the cantaloupe, then the coconuts, the skull-cracking sounds reverberating off the rocks, and I stood mesmerized as he split each sphere into two and then four and then eight and so on, and I could have continued standing there watching the transformation, perfect spheres rendered into irregular squares, when I caught sight of six brawny men approaching like a troop of macaques as they eyed the fruit from a distance. I quickly stepped forward and asked for a cup of diced coconut, another of cantaloupe, and a third of mango with lime and chili.

I would remain collected when I saw him again, pretend all was fine. I'd pretend it hadn't rankled, hadn't rankled at all, that he'd run in the opposite direction. I could even blame it on a greater force, make as though he were acting on orders from someone higher in command who dictated his movements, but no, he was responsible for his actions, and I, for that matter, for mine. And now that I thought about it, Tomás had simply accelerated a process that had already been set in motion. Perhaps it had started on the bus. I had fixated on the Joy Division songs and the languishing battery rather than the more pressing issue at hand. It was impossible to recall how those four syllables, Tomás Román, had once felt like an incantation, strong enough to hex school and city, the initials *TR* evoking the promise of something, two consonants awaiting a vowel awaiting an act. I finished my fruit while watching the bathers in the water, the curious way in which their legs disappeared into the waves until they became nothing but torsos, torsos afloat on the surface of the sea.

The bathers were exiting the water, each body gradually recovering its state of wholeness, when Tomás reappeared, dripping, at my side, his bathing trunks threatening to slide off his narrow hips. He raised an arm to shield his eyes from the reddish light of evening, from the reddish light or from anticipated anger or reproach. As casually as I could, I joked about his rusty inner compass, how it couldn't tell north from south and had set him, lightning speed, on the wrong course. He laughed nervously and said, No, no, no, without elaborating, then looked beyond me into the distance.

There in Oaxaca, dusk was announced not by the *tamalero*, nor by cobalt blue ceding to molten orange, but by the coral man, who would come into view just as the sun was departing. He was thin and malnourished as if plucked from the sea like his goods, all color and vital signs draining from him the longer he spent out of water. For sale were several black coral necklaces, twenty pesos apiece, and an assortment of polished chunks. More than once Tomás and I scanned the pieces and said no thank you, neither of us drawn to what lay in front of us. Neither of us was drawn to what lay in front of us, and after that day we began to go our separate ways.

NIGHT DOESN'T FALL, IT RISES, AND TWILIGHT IN
Zipolite was marked by a surge in activity. Some sought
the bar, others the bonfire. Tomás liked the bonfire, its
mellow tenor and roving guitar. For that reason and various others, I gravitated toward the bar. After so many
hours on the beach I welcomed a change in location, and
furthermore, the flames reminded me of the fire-eaters at
traffic lights in the city. These men would gulp down diesel
and once fueled up tilt back their heads, raise a lit torch to
their mouths, and roar out long, trembling flames, then
stumble over mutely to the car window and hold out a
hand for coins. I was reminded of them each time I saw a
bonfire, even when in the company of friendly Europeans
such as the Spanish merchant from Valencia who, when I
told him about the dwarfs, said his brothers were clowns

who had a double act, Polilla and Alcanfor, Moth and Mothball. Yet in the city, even when stopped at a traffic light, my thoughts would remain on green, and it was only in front of the fire, thrown into contemplative mode, that I'd think of these silent men, the flames like speech bubbles their only language.

Once the air cooled and the sun cast new patterns of glimmer on the water, I would head to the bar. I'd slip on my short dress or wraparound skirt and amble down the beach, past the bohemian glow of the bonfires, toward the lights and music. And it was at the bar one night, just as I was two-thirds through my second drink and debating what next, that I met the merman. It didn't take long for me to notice him in a corner, a ring of silence around him, his sharp Slavic features bringing a new geometry to the scene, and slanted eyes, almost reptilian, that drank in but didn't give out. His clothes seemed from elsewhere; snug black trousers of thin polyester that rode high at the waist and a white tank top and, even more oddly, a green cardigan, worn open—the temperature dropped a few degrees at night but never enough to warrant a sweater—topped off by navy-blue plastic sandals with one thick band across the top.

I'd seen him already, earlier that day, and witnessed something intimate enough that when I spotted him at the bar I felt I knew him just a little, although he clearly hadn't noticed me, so absorbed was he in his thoughts, so withdrawn from the general mood of the beach. All I could do was throw myself into his line of vision. After a slightly awkward approach, a few drops of cocktail splashed onto his table, I sat down, introduced myself, and asked his name, a question to which he simply smiled without providing an answer, clutching his bottle of beer and breathing calmly, evenly, at a different rhythm somehow from the rhythms around him. Each time he drank he'd wipe his mouth with the back of his hand and make a low guttural sound, and each time he did this I felt a sharp rise in desire, and after two or three minutes, possibly less, I knew I had found the person I wanted to be with, or at least the person to whom I would tell my story, here in Zipolite.

My eyes had initially been drawn that afternoon to his bathing trunks—high waist, mid thigh, green with a blue stripe down the side—which stood out from the other beachwear. I could tell the man had a handsome foreign face, at least through my sunglasses, at least from a distance. He was significantly older than me, in his mid to late thirties, or even early forties, and had light brown hair, longish at the front and shorn at the back, and a bit of a belly. Yet what interested me more than his pleasing appearance was that the man was building a sandcastle. Without drawing attention to myself I sat down about a meter and a half away, near a row of people spread out on towels, and from behind my sunglasses I began to observe the various stages that went into the construction.

Armed with a flat knife, bucket, and shovel, the man seemed oblivious to everyone on the beach, like a child in its sandbox he kept his focus within the parameters of his kingdom, and as he dug deep, setting the foundations, and piled high, hand stacking, patty-cake style, the great mound of wet sand, I couldn't help but feel that by the mere act of watching I was intruding on a childhood fear or fantasy, there in the design, as if one could read a person's past and future, homes real and imagined, in the way someone built their sandcastle.

Despite these thoughts, or because of them, I found it impossible to avert my eyes. After laying the foundations he smoothed out the surfaces with his knife, then packed and shaped, carved and smoothed some more, moistening at intervals. With large gentle hands he then built a tower and an arch, maintaining the knife at the same angle while cutting, always working, I noticed, from the highest point downward. And then came a bridge, and stairs spiraling around the tower and various doors and windows, some with ledges. Columns came next, creating wonderful shadows, and finally the roof, with inverted cone shapes like those in fairy tales. And the more the man worked on his sandcastle, the more sophisticated its architecture, the more I sensed the presence of the waves, rows of muscular men with interlocking arms that came closer in with each roll, as if they wanted his castle.

Every now and then the man would step away from his creation, presumably for a more panoramic view of the work in progress, and only at these moments would my eyes be drawn away from the castle to him, standing tall and casting a shadow, and from where I was sitting I could admire both the handsome profile of the man and the handsome profile of the castle against the horizon, its tones starting to deepen as people began their migration from beach to bar or hotel. Soon the structure was complete, just in time for the setting sun to lend it a preternatural glow, and the man brushed the sand off his legs and circled his creation. I could almost read his pride from afar as he studied it from every angle, occasionally leaning in to adjust one last detail, but then, then— I would never forget the sound of a sandcastle collapsing, the whoosh and the cry as the fine engineering work was erased within seconds—for, only minutes after finishing, he tripped over his shovel and fell into the castle, not into its center but into its right side, enough to topple the foundation. The towers went first, then the ramparts, the sculpted arch crumbled back into grains of sand, and with an air of defeat the man gave the bucket a kick, still unaware he was being observed, and trudged off, heels heavy in sand; it wasn't long after that the tide came in to finish the job and soon there was no trace whatsoever of either man or castle.

The merman may have been married, though he wore no wedding ring; he may have been a drug addict, though he had good teeth and flawless skin; he may have been a carpenter, train conductor, or physiotherapist. All I knew apart from the sandcastle was that he had a great stillness and could sit for ages without stirring, except for when he lifted his bottle of beer to his mouth to drink, then drying his lips with the back of his hand. And that his eyes were capable of considerable depth and expression as he watched and listened, his face mostly serious, almost idle, but with traces of livelier moments like oxidized swings at a playground. Yet he smiled whenever I did, and pulled faces when my tone turned solemn. Even if he didn't understand my words, I was reassured his concentration was such that he could read my mood and gauge my tone, that in itself was enough, and each time an atom of doubt flickered into my mind I had only to think back on the vision of him building his sandcastle. Yes, I had come to the beach, or rather run away, with Tomás, but it was clear there was no bond between us, and now the merman, I suspected, would make my journey worthwhile. It's often the case that one person leads you to another, at least that's what my experienced older cousin once told me, never write someone off since they may be the conduit, lead you to something more important than the original, and as the merman took quiet sips from his drink, I let the words tumble out.

There are two kinds of romantics, my older cousin had explained, the kind who is constantly falling in love and simply needs a person into whom they can pour every thought, dream, and project, and the kind of romantic who remains alone, waiting and waiting for the right person to arrive, a person who may not even exist. It was too early to know which kind I would be.

By the third night I stopped trying to guess which country the merman was from, or his mother tongue: there was no indication of nationality. I tried to read hints in his gestures but could only narrow it down to Europe, probably Eastern Europe, though I'd never met anyone from Eastern Europe before. And I didn't ask myself how he'd been able to travel; according to our history teacher, most people living behind the Iron Curtain weren't allowed to travel to the West unless they were gymnasts or chess players. And I also had no idea where he was staying, whether in a palapa or a bungalow or a nearby hotel, he would simply show up at the bar each evening and leave a couple of hours later. I didn't know his name, so I called him the merman: mermen can hail from any country, speak any language, and look like anything, and there was something about him that rang of half land, half sea, as if he belonged to both but was hesitant to commit to either.

At a certain point the merman would push away his empty bottle, rise from his chair, and smile, polite yet distant, distant enough to suggest it was good night rather than a suggestion to accompany him. After he left I would wait a few minutes and then stumble down the beach and,

after so many drinks, collapse in my hammock. The merman was generous and always paid; the moment I'd finish
a drink he would raise his hand to signal to the waiter and
with a looping gesture ask for two more, and whenever
the time came to pay the merman would again raise a
hand and push away mine if it happened to be holding
money, and from a miniature cloth bag hanging from his
neck he would extract a few coins and tightly folded bills,
counting too softly for me to hear in what language, furthermore the music from the bar drowned out the mur-
muring although we always sat at the table farthest from
the speakers.

Each time the waiter brought our drinks he would deliver
the bottle of beer with a lime sliced in two on the side,
and each time the merman would make a sign to say he
did not want the lime, only the beer, but the very next
time the waiter appeared with our order he would again
bring a lime sliced in two, its halves still connected by a
hinge, and then take it away again, only to bring the same
lime back to the table forty-five minutes later. Though the
merman seemed like a patient sort, not easily ruffled, I'd
notice his mouth twitch whenever the waiter arrived with
the same lime. I would try to think of something to say
to distract him from this irritating repetition, but the one
night it didn't happen (there was another waiter working,
who wasn't offering limes with beer), the merman looked
as if something were missing.

I decided I should tell him about Tomás, and why I found myself on the beach in the first place, though I said it was mostly because of the dwarfs, twelve Ukrainian dwarfs on the run from a Soviet circus touring Mexico, rather than the ruse it had, truthfully, been. I'd seen the note in the paper myself, I explained, there in the bottom right-hand corner of the page emitting its own radioactive glow, and it was this story that had set everything in motion. In fact the newspaper clipping was still in my bag, ready to be brought out should someone not believe me, and besides, I was prone to losing things and if one day it were to go astray the information would've at least been transferred to a few memories. Already the paper had become vulnerable along the lines where it had been folded, somewhere between the description of the empty trailer and the speculation over Oaxaca, marking the path that led off the page and into the wilds of Mexico. I watched as the merman's faraway eyes ran over the words without any obvious sign of comprehension or surprise; it was possible that for him this sort of news item wasn't of interest, maybe in his country dwarfs ran away from circuses every month, and who cared that it had happened in Mexico; different laws govern different geographies.

As he studied the clipping I leaned closer in, my head almost touching his, and inhaled a humid union of brine and pine. I was trying to establish which scent was dominant, that of the sea or his cologne, when he returned the article, pushed away his beer, and rose from the table, reminding me of his not insignificant height, and with a semi-wave announced he was now leaving, and shuffled off in his blue plastic sandals. The first night I'd been taken aback by his abrupt departure but there he was again on the second night, and the third, and I stopped worrying about whether I would see him as he was always there, installed at the same table at the back of the bar clutching his Sol or Negra Modelo. And once he departed I would return to my hammock, Tomás nowhere in sight, and try to sleep, exposed to the elements, to snatches of conversation from passing shadows, and the whir and lull of giant insects.

ANOTHER DAY: ANOTHER STRIP OF SAND, CLUSTER OF trees, band of waves, band of sky. The beach continued to look like a naïve composition, still waiting for a pair of scissors to come and disturb it. And there was the hut, for instance, in a new position, a modest cutout, pale blue against the other blues. At night it looked like a cardboard box a child had left behind. I never saw anyone emerge from it, but the woman at El Cósmico explained that the Zipolite lifeguard, a robust woman in her fifties, lived inside, and since the structure was on wheels she could move from spot to spot and through its windows keep an eye on the water.

One afternoon not far from the hut I spotted a group of people lying on the sand, three on their backs and two on their stomachs. I couldn't help but fear they were victims of some nautical calamity; their positions looked wrong, crooked, arms and legs jutting out at awkward angles as though they'd been cast out of the hut like dice, or else washed ashore by the waves, left to the chance of the ocean's directives, a random throw that had created this perturbing configuration. I was debating whether to raise the alarm when someone's beach ball struck one of the motionless bodies, the impact of which made the woman jump up in her black-and-white polka-dot bikini and shake a fist and start yelling in Italian, addressing an imprecise spot in the air since the owner of the ball, most likely intimidated, failed to materialize. Her yells ricocheted off the dozing bodies of her companions, two boys, a girl, and a man, who sprang up jack-in-the-box, and soon everyone was awake, and incontestably alive.

Sometimes when I shut my eyes I imagined the dwarfs vaulting forward and backward on the waves. I couldn't lose sight of them, at least not in my thoughts. Perhaps one of them had broken away from the group and was standing amid the buses in the terminal's back alley, still in his makeup, with arched eyebrows and overstated mouth; or walking along a dusty road clenching a cigarette and a bunch of flowers as trucks ten times his size barreled past; or sitting in a *fonda* eating tacos while drivers jeered at him from another table; or returning to the dusty road, hands in pockets, a stray dog barking at his shadow. As the beach became more crowded, voices clinking all around me, a happier picture rose to mind: that of the dwarfs in a village plaza dancing to "Dios Nunca Muere," my parents' favorite waltz. And then a longer-lasting scenario of happiness: that after days and days of travel, the dwarfs had arrived at a hamlet somewhere deep inland, stepping out of the cornfields and looking so sad and tired that the native women rushed to feed them. Over the course of the meal they would tell their story, primarily through gestures—the only languages at hand Spanish, Zapotec, Russian, and Ukrainian: misery in the grip of a ruthless ringmaster, flight from the circus, journey. Once everyone had finished eating, the villagers, also mainly through gestures, would extend an invitation: the dwarfs were welcome to join their community as long as they contributed however they could, either with manual labor or entertainment or ideally both, and the dwarfs would accept and remain forever in this hamlet pocketed away somewhere in the depths of Mexico.

It was during a moment of such musing that the growl of a motor shredded my thoughts, and the sound patterns of beach and ocean. I sat up just as two *lanchas*, simple boats with low sides and noisy motors, were surging past a few meters from the shore. Each was steered by a *lanchero* accompanied by his handful of passengers, some of whom anxiously gripped the sides of the boat. A few bathers in the water quickly paddled out of their way. Once the boats clattered off, their obtrusive presence absorbed back into the greater whole, I spotted Tomás near a yellow flag, his head bobbing up and down in the waves. He seemed to be looking over. I made a sign and he began wading out, not without effort since the water was rowdy, extra swell probably added by the departing boats, but after a minute or so he was at my side, dripping and salted, his face a pinkish red, his hair like a melted helmet. Come back, jaunty figure in black, come back. But my affections had started to gravitate elsewhere so what did I care whether the person from the city was another on the coast? It was the discrepancy that came back to nag me, this rare transformation, rather than the situation itself.

Seeing he had no towel, I offered him mine.

I was thinking of wandering down to the nearest village, he said, patting his face dry. Wanna come?

Sure. A change of scenery would be great. As a matter of fact, I'd give anything for a change of scenery.

But this is what beach holidays are about, you know, soothing monotony rather than variation, each day at the beach is meant to be the same, that's what makes it relaxing, it's the monotony that helps you unwind.

I shrugged, and asked him to wait while I fetched my bag and sandals. How could I explain that in my family we had never gone to a hot place to idle around on the grass or the sand—in my family, vacations weren't about that, they always involved going to another city and taking in culture, I wasn't used to monotony, in fact had no idea what to do with it, free time was like a useless toy in my hand.

The journey down the dirt road was memorable not for the landscape or the conversation but because of the hundreds of two-dimensional toads that were strewn across our path. Large and haunchless, the creatures had been run over by cars and then crisped by the sun, lugubrious dots connecting beach to town, and I avoided them as we walked along. Tomás began whistling a tune. Before I could guess what it was, a silver Suburban came charging down the road. We jumped out of its way just in time. Through the rolled-down windows a cumbia blared out, the notes of clarinet, congas, and timpani left hanging in the air, and for a split second I thought I caught sight of several heads low in the seats. But the vehicle sped past too quickly for me to be sure, angry clouds of dust in its wake.

Once the Suburban had faded in the distance my attention was brought back to the toads. The sight of them continued to unnerve me, made worse by the crackling each time Tomás stepped down on one, for every now and then he went out of his way to do so. The sound reminded me of the mummies of Guanajuato, where I'd been the year before with my parents. After a visit to the Don Quijote museum we'd gone to see the mummies from an abandoned mining town—more than a hundred of them, condemned to wear their death in public after being exhumed in the nineteenth century owing to a burial tax few families could afford to pay. The particular condition of the subsoil had preserved them, and once above ground the dry mountain air had continued the job. They were a horrific sight, with their void eyes and frozen screams, and now that I listened to Tomás trample the toads, I felt certain that treading on a mummy from that museum would have sounded similar.

The village was small. Shriveled, almost, by the sun. One central building combined bank, post office, police station, doctor, hairdresser, and grocery—basic services any community would require, according to a sign. Next door crouched a two-story hotel, its coarse pink stone pocked as if by years of affliction. According to Tomás the place was crawling with drug dealers who did business on the beach by day and returned there after dark. I peered into the lobby half expecting to find a shady foursome bent over a deck of cards but all I saw was a young bellhop in sandals. I was seized by the impulse to call my parents and let them know I was fine, that I was fine and would be heading home before long, I didn't know when, exactly, but certainly before the end of the month. As I stalled outside, composing the conversation in my head, Tomás nipped my arm and asked why I'd stopped.

I want to make a quick call and tell my parents I'm okay.

You're crazy.

Just a few words.

Luisa, it's a terrible idea. They'll be able to trace it . . .

And so I walked on, though part of me remained outside those two buildings imagining their instruments of communication, instruments that could have reconnected me to my parents however briefly, a few instants to transmit my voice and with it some sort of reassurance, and even once I was sitting with Tomás at a table at La Tortuga, a lone restaurant at the intersection of two sloping streets, even once we'd crossed its outer mantle of hanging plastic beads, entered the room furnished rustic-style and ordered from the showcase exhibiting the dishes of the day, for the most part silver-streaked corpses whose flowing sea had recently been turned into a bed of rice, and I'd asked for every vegetable dish on the menu, which amounted to three, even then I felt tugged back to the hotel and the offices beside it.

Tropical music piped out of two corner speakers as we waited for our food. The curtain of plastic beads made a commotion as a fat woman with shopping bags lumbered in and plunked herself down at another table, joined minutes later by two noisy families, their presence announced by raucous children and the smoke of exotic cigarettes. By the time our food arrived, even the afternoon breeze had entered.

As Tomás ate his fish, noisily punctuated by suction sounds whenever he paused to drink from his beer, I considered mentioning how he had run off the other day. I could have asked whether it was the cosmos exerting its pull, pulling him in another direction, toward people who also responded to its call. But each time I was on the verge of saying something I held back; there was no point in reproaching him for acting out interiors.

My father has always said that most photographs taken in public contain a ghost, that unknown person who crops up seconds before the button is pressed, a foreign body that floats in and binds its image to yours for eternity. Toward the end of the meal I turned to see that the mother of one family was photographing her two girls and I happened to be sitting directly behind them, in the camera's line of vision. Now that I thought of it, I'd most likely appeared in some of the pictures taken at the Burroughs house by the boy from San Francisco, upon developing the roll back home he'd found me there in the background with my head full of daydream, my image now linked forever to his documentation of that space.

I asked for the bill and told Tomás I felt like returning to the beach. He too seemed ready. This time we took a shorter route, yet similarly littered with dried toads. The road also happened to be dotted with squashed fruit that had fallen from the trees, each piece mobbed by excited ants that made the lifeless toads seem even more lifeless.

Once back at the beach Tomás introduced me to his new friend Mario, a Zipolitan with long white hair tied back in a straggly ponytail and a voice that suggested he'd smoked every herb in the vicinity. They had met over a bonfire, Tomás said, and got along instantly. Mario had a dubious air about him, I couldn't help thinking, yet Tomás hung on his every word, especially when he began speaking of a *tropicalization of the spirit*, that's what Mario called it, at the beach you just had to tropicalize, he had said to me when we'd been introduced, as if to suggest I was guilty of resisting. The man talked and talked, he talked without filters, letting the words pour out without ever stopping to consider what he was saying, and yet he spoke so much that every now and then he would say something mean-ingful, the words simply aligned themselves in such a way that even he seemed surprised by the profound declaration he had just uttered, and this spontaneous wisdom was what probably impressed Tomás.

After watching them walk off I decided, despite my reservations, that the time had finally come to obey the ocean's call. Nudity was optional, I reminded myself, yet that afternoon I surprised myself by conceding halfway. I never expected to but found it oddly natural; after all, the only way of becoming someone else was to ignore the voices that spoke up, alarmed and protesting, as I pulled off my T-shirt, unwrapped my skirt, and unhooked my bra. If I deliberated I would reverse, so without giving it another thought I ran into the water, the sea as warm as the air, and let myself wade in up to my waist. I closed my eyes, slightly aroused by the water's embrace, its invisible arms wrapping around my legs, and asked myself where the merman was at that hour. Maybe he too was in the ocean, at a different point along, and we were connected by the same waves that brushed my body and then his. I thought of the homeless woman bathing in the fountain, such a strange sight, half troubling, half magnificent, the water adding ripples to her age; who knew whether the water in Zipolite added or subtracted, but either way, I felt revived.

Revived, that is, until I happened to gaze into the horizon without end and felt its vastness begin to swallow me; if I stayed in much longer I was certain I would dissolve, there were probably hundreds of dissolved bodies in the ocean, swirling around with the shells and seaweed, that's what happens when you immerse yourself too fully in any vastness, you eventually become part of it, part of the landscape, quite literally. The undertow was growing rougher. I started back to shore, pushing against the water, which seemed to have acquired more will and density, and only then noticed the cautionary yellow flag in the distance, flapping on its stalk.

On my way out of the ocean I encountered a fat man with satyr eyes, his parts so immense I couldn't help staring as he waded ahead with a woman, also corpulent, in tow, her green panties clinging to her curves, her breasts like hefty church bells. As they too waded out, thighs thrusting against the water, the woman threw her arms around the man's belly, and once ashore they trudged off leaving sensual dents in the sand, their bulk somehow undiminished by the perspective of distance.

Sand, towel, safety. The threat of a devouring vastness was soon replaced, however, by the burden of the more concrete. As I lay there, the image of the hotel building rose to mind, and the number of telephones I must have walked past, and the call I could have made yet hadn't. My lamentations were cut short by a presence by my head. I sat up to examine the visitor, its palette bold against the coastal tones: a long body sheathed in iridescent chain mail, a crest extending from head to tail in a ridge of spikes, a massive head like a crowned Eastern deity. Here beside me sat an iguana, its torpor undermined by the occasional blink and almost imperceptible quiver of its jowls and the dewlap under its chin as it collected the sun's warmth. Its mouth hung open, just enough to reveal two rows of minuscule pointy teeth, and its pupils seemed fixed on me. I closed my eyes and tried to ignore its stare but could feel it through my lids. There was purpose in those eyes, something beyond mere curiosity, and I couldn't help suspecting the iguana had been sent by my parents to spy.

I thought back on the party at Diego Deán's, on his three iguanas who sat dignified in their tanks observing the somewhat undignified dance around them, and now on the sand I began to feel in the grip of a similar nervous energy. Nowhere near as strung out as that night, naturally, but enough to cancel out the mood that'd started to set in. Seeing this iguana, which had in the last few minutes vanished back into its hermetic world, left me troubled. I willed time to accelerate and for the sun to dissolve into a thin fiery line. I wanted to see the merman, I wanted to have a few drinks. That was the moment when I untensed, at the bar at night, distanced from the beach and its stories, but evening was still a whole concept away. I tried to think of something neutral. The posters in my room: Siouxsie Sioux in a feathery headdress; a sepia Emiliano Zapata with saber, rifle, sash, and sombrero; the Caspar David Friedrich of two moon gazers, beside a photograph I once took of Caifanes playing at La Quiñonera. Perhaps they'd all grown discolored or were curling up at the edges. No, not that quickly. Yet surely it's the intensity of an absence that counts, not its length. Something must have changed, the room must look different, something must complain.

AT NIGHT THE BEACHCOMBERS WOULD EMERGE, slow-moving silhouettes entirely oblivious to the rest of us as they set out on their mission. At first I didn't know who they were, these two dark figures roaming the shore, their flashlights directed at the stretch of sand in front of them, until I heard the woman at El Cósmico discussing them with one of her customers, an inquisitive man seated at the next table. He too had seen them, and asked her to explain. They are Horacio Gómez and Serpentino Hernández, she replied, Zipolite's beachcombers. The sand stole but it also bestowed, safeguarding objects until the sun went down, and these men were determined to find the coins, watches, sunglasses, and other trinkets that had been left behind. Horacio was the much older man, and Serpentino therefore the younger and more successful beachcomber, with sharper vision, and each night the two would meet by a certain boulder with their flashlights and start combing the sand for treasure, rarely entering into conversation, or knowing much about each other despite being colleagues. But the woman at El Cósmico knew a few details, and couldn't resist sharing them. Horacio had been to the city only four times in his life, and his wife had died many years ago. As for Serpentino, his wife lived up north and he saw her every Christmas; he had a handsome face, you could say classical, but was missing a considerable number of teeth, in fact his mouth resembled an empty cave with stalactites and stalagmites. His dream was to save up enough money to buy a metal detector, but the older beachcomber greatly disapproved of that idea.

And yet I only saw these men from afar, they never came into focus, they remained patches of ink in the background, sometimes still, sometimes in motion, sometimes vertical, sometimes bent over at forty-five degrees, sometimes one wore a hat, sometimes one used a cane. I was struck by this profession driven by optimism, by the thought that there was always something to discover if you only looked, but as far as I could tell the main items to be found were smoked-down joints and cigarettes, empty bottles and marine debris, in fact a museum of debris, none of it the exciting flotsam and jetsam that might wash up on other shores.

Meanwhile the ocean continued to write and rewrite its long ribbon of foam, changing the contours of Tomás's drawing, adjusting and readjusting, moving them backward and forward. It was a quarter past crow, half past seagull, five to owl. I could roughly gauge time from the movement of the sun yet the hour of the day and the day of the week seemed irrelevant, one folding into the next like a collapsing accordion, and I felt no need to distinguish between them. I'd intentionally left my watch at home, or perhaps I'd forgotten it, but what purpose, anyway, would it serve here on the beach—Oaxaca ran on Oaxaca time, Tomás on Tomás time, even the dogs ran on their own time, one punctuated by hunger, naps, and observation, the metronome skipping a beat whenever there was a new sound or smell in the offing. At night I would think back on what a pious aunt once said when I mentioned I found it hard to believe in any higher power—she had gazed at me with a look of pity she didn't attempt to hide before describing the solitude of the atheist. As an atheist you are unaccompanied, you see, at night you close the door and have no one to turn to, whereas she felt accompanied continually; wherever she was, whatever she was doing, there was always someone watching, a divine witness to her life. Not a particularly attractive thought, I remembered thinking, but instead I felt compelled to agree with her, even join in her commiseration over my barren spirit.

• • •

There are days, indeed whole weeks, in life that seem nocturnal. Some lives could be mapped out entirely via nocturnal scenes, and once we had firmly entered evening, the bar would beckon. The bar beckoned, and the merman wore many rings. He hadn't worn them on the day of the sandcastle, I would have noticed the glint, but he wore them to the bar each night, and often while I was speaking he would fiddle with them, three on one hand, two on the other. Four were silver bands and the fifth was the head of a wolf, its snout pointing outward as if on permanent watch; he wore this ring on the middle finger of his left hand, and I'd steal glances at it in an attempt to determine its significance. In his country wolves might have special meaning, or maybe he was a member of a wolf club, but no, I decided, the merman was a lone wolf, like this solitary ring snarling amid the nondescript bands, and if I hadn't already named him merman I would have searched for a more lupine moniker. But in Zipolite, I now understood, one could be many things at once.

One night, apart from the quiet miracle of the merman, there happened to be a DJ visiting from Berlin, a redhead who'd crossed the ocean with his tunes, songs I much preferred to the frolicsome beach anthems thus far. Yet most people didn't seem as captivated by the music, and there were fewer bodies in the improvised area of the dance floor. When the DJ put on a Kraftwerk song, I grabbed the merman's hand. At first he resisted, so ensconced in his stillness, but I didn't relent and after a few more tugs I got him to follow me to a slightly tenebrous patch of the palapa and there we began to dance, the merman tense and uncertain, so I took both his hands and led as best I could, surprised to see that the merman, so graceful and composed when seated, seemed to lack all coordination, shuffling jerkily, almost mechanically, his shoulders twitching like a cement mixer as he lurched from side to side.

When the next song came on, Camouflage's "The Great Commandment," the merman placed his hands on my shoulders and drew me to him. Without a second thought I rested my head against the ribbed cotton of his tank top, closed my eyes, and breathed in the heady scents of sea and cologne. We stayed in this position for the duration of the next track as well, enormous arms enfolding my torso as guitar riffs vibrated off his chest. Eyes still shut, and completely engulfed, I let myself be carried back to nights at El Nueve, to its grotto of European moonlight, and imagined we were there, the merman and I, moving in circles around the DJ booth, everyone from Adán the Aviator to the Scottish Goth making way for us, the regal couple who cut a swath across the room, silencing everyone with our great romance. My thoughts transported us so fully to Londres in the Zona Rosa that I began to fret over what I would do with the merman once the night was over. I couldn't bring him home just like that, nor could I release him into the city, especially if he didn't speak our language; yes, it was going to be a problem once the night ended. This imaginary dilemma began to occupy my thoughts, burrowing deeper as the song wore on, until I opened my eyes and saw Tomás.

He was standing in front of me, in front of us. Floppy hair and baggy white shorts, a rip in the shoulder of his T-shirt. Stock-still amid the dancing figures, in every way looking deflated, he stood and stared, at me, at the merman, then back at me. Merman, meet Fantômas. The merman frowned and released me, cocking his head as if to ask who this was. This is the friend I mentioned, I said above the music, and whispered to Tomás to go away. He didn't so much as blink an eye so I pulled him aside and asked him again to leave, couldn't he see we were immersed in conversation, to which he gave me a baffled look, aware, possibly, that we hadn't been speaking and if we had, it would have been one-way and in a language only one of us could understand. He glanced over at the merman, who had left the dance floor and was on his way back to our table. I only came to check on you, Tomás shrugged, I wanted to make sure you were okay. Of course I'm okay, I replied coldly. For a few seconds we stood staring at each other without exchanging a word. And then he shrugged a second time, and walked off.

The merman's manner grew even more reserved now that someone had adjourned our moment of intimacy, and back at the table I clarified yet again, in case he'd missed it, that this was the friend with whom I'd come in search of the dwarfs. I confessed I'd been interested in him at first, initially it had been some sort of romance . . . But that was the problem with mysterious people, I explained, once you spend time with them they're not so mysterious after all, and as I said this the merman smiled, as if promising, no matter what, to remain a mystery.

The Hyades set in the evening, and
Taurus begins to rise.
Vega rises in the evening, and
in the morning the Pleiades and the Hyades start to rise.

The Antikythera Mechanism had charted what appeared
at sunset, what withdrew from the dawn sky. Despite the
electrical currents provided by the merman and the more
or less tacit understanding I'd arrived at with Tomás, there
were reminders that my nerves remained raw. Regardless
of how hard I tried, I couldn't ignore the occasional mirage
of my parents hovering in the background, because that's
what parents do, they hover, whether in person or from a
distance, and even when freed of giant math instruments
you will always have, at the back of your thoughts, hover-

ing parents, and no position can entirely shake them off. I'll be home before long, I told them in my mind, despite having no idea as to *how* long. I did not want to travel on my own, nor did I want to abandon the merman.

Often I'd lie restless on a towel or in the hot shallow grave of the sand, keeping an eye on the flag—green, yellow, or red. I would think of the Zapotec girls, wondering on what stretch of beach, exactly, their corpses had been laid out. In front of El Cósmico, isn't that what the woman had said, but I could no longer remember more. Sometimes I'd try the come-and-go shade of the palm trees, avoiding the hammock by day as I would my bed in the city. All my life I'd shunned naps, they only brought empty feelings and disorientation, and as for the hammock, suspension is a dubious state, stability impossible if nothing is touching the ground. So I let my nerves be frayed, at times probably indulged them. I just couldn't imagine relaxing one hundred percent, and just to guarantee I kept a grip on things and didn't let down my guard or allow matters to get too picturesque, I held on to the one book I'd brought with me, Lautréamont's *Les Chants de Maldoror.*

Every now and then I would dip in, as I would in the city, and each time its angry spume jumped out and spat in my face, but I felt stronger having it in my hands. After all, Mr. Berg had given him especially to *me*, he hadn't assigned him to the rest of the class—too savage, he'd said, for the others—Lautréamont was mine, and mine alone, and I was closer to him than anyone else on the beach, of that I was certain. Isidore Ducasse was my ally in Zipolite, and everything I knew about him made me like him even more. There was a shortage of biographical facts, Berg had warned me, yet I savored those he mentioned. Lautréamont/Ducasse was cranky and taciturn, and kept his distance from everyone. He hardly ate but drank vast amounts of coffee and suffered from migraines. During the day he would wander up and down the banks of the Seine and then stay up all night writing as he pounded the keys of a piano in search of phrases and rhythms. The flora and fauna of his native Montevideo, where he'd spent his childhood, crept into many a frame. In Paris he lived in a hotel and was so anonymous that when he died, aged twenty-four, the death certificate was signed by the hotel manager and valet. And, of course, the fact of only one surviving photograph, a final act of defiance. I would open *Maldoror* and imbibe a few words—certain ones in particular were good for the arsenal: *foul, lewdness, torture, vampire, ignominious, blood, saliva, sinews*—and continue with my day; even a quick visit to the pages was enough to set my nerves on edge, but also steel them.

The other students at COCA had their bodyguards. And I, courtesy of Mr. Berg, had Lautréamont. With him I had no need for anyone at school, once Etienne left it was parched land, and I kept the book in my bag at all times. It might've been a case of the howler monkey imitating the jaguar's roar, but with this sort of ally I felt more powerful than the bodyguards, an absurdity of daily life that at the beach seemed even more absurd. It was probably true that whenever one looked back at life in the city, particularly from a place lacking in city features, a great deal would seem absurd. But few details, from the vantage point of Oaxaca, seemed as ridiculous to me now as the bodyguards, or *guaruras*, particularly those that gathered around our school, a mass of black circling the campus like dense planetary rings, the density reiterated by the cars they drove, faceless black and platinum SUVs with windows as tinted as the sunglasses they wore.

The men added local color, or rather shadow, to the street, and the last time I saw them was right before I left for Oaxaca. After class I had exited through the main entrance rather than walking to the parking lot to catch the school bus, and not only that, but a few minutes before the bell since PE had ended early. And there they were, fanned out by the gates awaiting their charges. Some were puffing on cigarettes, others had gathered around the taco stand that had been set up for them. I was off their radar, however, subsumed into the hectic panorama, and their eyes passed over my being the same way they'd pass over a tree or a gate. I always felt so insignificant when in front of these men, not only the ones at school but others throughout the city, although bodyguards elsewhere at least registered my presence with a microgesture, whereas the ones outside school showed no sign whatsoever of acknowledging I was there.

But that day had been different. I no longer felt diminished by the *guaruras* or the world they represented, soon I would be far from it, and as I stared into the tinted glasses of one man by the sizzling taco stand, I was convinced he was staring back at me. Someone had noticed that here was a female student exuding a burlier kind of energy.

An old shoe shiner arrived with his son. I'd seen them before, these humble entrepreneurs who would materialize with wooden crates that folded out like concertinas, their music an arrangement of rags, brushes, and jars of polish. The son also carried a stool. As soon as they'd settled in, there would always be one watchdog who'd break off from duty to have his shoes shined, five minutes of feeling solemn and important while a man knelt at his feet.

At two thirty, the bell—a sign for the shoe shiner and his son to put away their implements, and for the taco man to turn off his griddle and draw the shutter. From that moment onward, all attention was directed elsewhere, every head turned in the direction of the gates, and through the sea of black I noticed a ripple of nervous tics, *guaruras* were prone to them, as the kids began to pour out. I couldn't help thinking of how differently each of us inhabited the pavement, as we would no doubt inhabit the world beyond. That day I no longer felt inferior. Well, I had never truly felt inferior yet sometimes found myself acting as though I did, that was the effect these people had on you, even if you existed outside their sphere you still formed part of the hierarchy, were somehow implicated. That afternoon I threw a quick glance, impervious, as the hulking men went up to the little people and relieved them of their bags before ushering them into the haughty vehicles.

I now tried to access some of what I'd experienced that day on the cusp of my trip, to resummon a few particles of exhilaration, remind myself of how powerful I had felt walking toward Constituyentes, where I boarded the Ruta 100 bus that took me to the terminal, and even during mood-menacing moments while Tomás and I awaited our departure, even then I had felt indomitable, poised to leap out of myself and into another.

AT THE FIRST HINTS OF SUNDOWN I HEADED TO THE bar, arriving at our table minutes before the merman. I saw his face appear beside a column of the palapa, survey the scene, and then break into a smile, faint yet fond, as he walked over. That evening, no cardigan: the white tank top allowed for his muscled arms to come into relief, and also highlighted the chest against which I'd pressed my head, a few hairs emerging but thankfully not too many. That evening I didn't speak much and instead joined him in his silence, a comfortable silence eased along by drinks and music, and by the frequent exchange of glances that made me long for more. But the more I longed, the more timid I grew. As if sensing my inhibition the merman pushed aside our drinks and reached out and touched my hand, caressed it once and for no more than a few seconds, but in doing so he raised the wattage.

At that moment a metallic-blue fly came buzzing into his face. He waved it away and took a sip of beer. Before long the insistent insect zoomed past again and landed on the table, its movements soon curtailed by the sticky residue. Tiny feet struggled to lift off, the antennae went berserk, wings fluttered anxiously. An impossible feat to detach itself from the surface. I observed the little bundle of panic and considered coming to its rescue, in fact had already removed the straw from my cocktail and just sucked out the remaining drops of tequila sunrise, when the merman's fist came pounding down and reduced the fly to the black smudge of an instant. Then, more delicately, he picked up the remains between two fingers, opened his mouth, and flung it in. Whatever the fly had been collecting—sand, dirt, experience—was swallowed down. A queer chuckle, then back to serious. I smiled nervously, a bit horrified, and debated whether I still wanted to kiss the mouth that had just eaten a fly. In any case, there was no need for debate, since the merman wiped his lips with the back of his hand and rose from his seat, offering his usual goodbye, the half arc of a wave, and with something close to relief I watched his tall figure cut through the bar and disappear into the night.

As usual the ocean was restless, a counterpoint of white crests and dark moving hills, and one could see, almost feel, the spray from afar. Once in my hammock I thought about the fly and its aborted journey. And of the merman's gesture: anger, joke, or provocation? The overhead lamp burned out, its ghostly white moths departed. I say burned out but in truth each palapa was run by a woman, usually of large physique, who dictated its mood via the main lamp overhead. Wick or filament, that'd been the question, until one day I'd discovered a pile of wires, a coil of current connected to the lamps overhead, and I couldn't help concluding that each palapa was to some extent deftly choreographed by its woman, a secret production manager who observed from behind a screen before deciding on the right level of illumination.

I shut my eyes, opened them, shut, reopened, readying myself for an even deeper black. But each time I reopened them I could still see the outlines of items around me, Tomás's empty hammock, the wooden beams overhead, more clearly than night usually allowed. I leaned out and gazed up at the sky, and there I discovered another light source, far more constant and powerful than any lamp. A ripe, dazzling moon, the kind I'd seen in picture books as a child. I asked myself how I hadn't noticed it earlier, this commanding presence in the sky. Yet my grand view was soon marred by the sound of the waves, they seemed louder with every roll, why was it that people always found it so peaceful, in every shop there were recordings of waves washing over more waves, it was a mystery how that eerie disembodied sound could lead anyone to sleep, though it's true that in the city when city noises kept me awake I would pretend the traffic was the tide, and that night in

Zipolite I reversed the illusion and envisioned the waves as a steady stream of cars, coming toward me and receding.

I was considering getting up again, even returning to the bar for one more drink, when I heard a high-pitched voice, a voice speaking a language I didn't recognize, remote from the cadence of Spanish and the indigenous tongues of Oaxaca. The words had a gentle ring to them, soft vowel sounds each cushioned by a *sshh*, and the hum of a *dzzz* here and there like a bee pollinating the sentence. I strained my ears to catch every syllable. A second voice, in the same language and nearly as high, joined in. I quietly sat up and tried to keep my hammock from swaying. Standing a few feet away, their silhouettes poignant against the moon, were two small figures, about as tall as children, in baggy garments. They had come to a halt and one of them was pointing up into the sky. A gush of admiration, more words uttered in the strange tongue, and then they vanished.

Tomás didn't believe me the next morning. For once he was there, curled up in his hammock, immobilized by a hangover. When I told him what I'd seen, that I'd seen two of the dwarfs, he mumbled something, threw an arm across his face, and rolled over. I stood by his hammock and shook the cords, repeating what I'd said, how could my words not produce more of a reaction, but he only groaned. I had no choice but to search for them on my own. What else was there to do, and besides, the only reason I'd wanted Tomás along was because he was familiar with the geography and four eyes are better than two. I was certain I had seen them, a full moon is nearly ten times brighter than the quarter phase, and my ears hadn't fooled me either, I'd viewed enough news clips and movies to recognize the sound of Russian or something akin.

After a quick visit to El Cósmico, the coffee unexpectedly bitter that morning, I scoured the beach for signs, finding meaning in a set of hammocks hanging unusually low to the ground and a procession of mini-footsteps that led toward the sea. Down by the rocks I spotted three blond figures in old-fashioned swimming trunks, but when I ran over they turned into European children with their nanny. More figures hunched over a chessboard turned out to be twin brothers enjoying a game of checkers. In other words, the dwarfs were everywhere and nowhere, and after a few hours my energy began to wane.

That evening I could hardly wait to meet the merman, to tell him what I'd seen, two figures speaking a language that was foreign to me but possibly not to him, two *small* figures, staring up at the moon in joint contemplation, scarcely a vision one would anticipate at the beach, especially glimpsed from one's hammock. I arrived at the bar with the first striations of dusk and claimed our table at the back, people starting to trickle in as the music gradually mounted in beats and volume, but no sign of the merman. A pair of dogs entered, looked around, and left. I fetched a drink and eventually a second, scanning each face. One hour went by. Another. I decided to pace my drinking but soon gave in and tried the local blue cocktail. The fabulists from my first few nights had all left, either migrated to other beaches or gone off to carry out their missions, and the new conversations around me sounded too dull to pursue.

By ten o'clock I was running out of cash and patience, and the blue cocktail with its disintegrating olives had tasted like aquarium. When a man with thin lips and curly hair offered to buy me a drink, I accepted. What was I doing on my own, he inquired, to which I replied I was waiting for my boyfriend. After bringing me my drink he fetched his from another table and helped himself to the free seat by my side. He then asked what I was doing at the beach. I replied that apart from being on holiday *with my boyfriend* I was searching for a troupe of Ukrainian dwarfs. Did you say Ukrainian? Yes, they defected from a Soviet circus that had been touring Mexico. I gave no details, only the headline, but the headline alone was enough to send the man into a tizzy, and in this sudden state of agitation he informed me that he worked part-time at the Trotsky House in Mexico City, soon to be turned into a museum on the fiftieth anniversary of his death. A deep flush that had begun in his face quickly extended to his words as he explained how shaken he was by the thought of Ukrainian nationals at large in our land, who knew where the situation might lead, and after three attempts at lighting his cigarette he told me that Mexico had been the very first country on the American continent to establish relations with the USSR in 1924, and then President Cárdenas had welcomed Trotsky in 1936; well, that was fine, but then Mexico entered World War II by declaring war on the Axis powers and cozying up to the Soviet Union, was I even aware of that, and then continued without waiting for a reply, so who knew what might happen now that these Ukrainian nationals were on the loose, Mexico was surely a haven for Soviet spies because of its location, so close to the United States and so far from everywhere else, in fact he'd heard that Mexican officials allowed the KGB to carry out its operations in our country, indeed many of the personnel at the Soviet Embassy were agents working undercover as chauffeurs, clerks, and diplomats, did I know what the KGB was, the man asked. Yes, I nodded, and he paused for a moment to finish off his drink and his cigarette before offering some final thoughts. Who better to go around collecting confidential information, prying their way into people's innermost worlds, than circus performers? He wondered whether they'd been preparing for years, whether they secretly knew Spanish. Whether they were, or could become, significant pawns in a larger political game. Whether they had anything to do with the 17,000 tons of powdered milk contaminated by Chernobyl fallout that was on the verge of being distributed across Mexico earlier that year before the whistle was blown. Whether . . . *¡Jorge, qué haces, ven aquí!* His speculation was cut short by a woman in a flowered dress. The man excused himself and slunk off.

If the conversation had gone in another direction I might have told him that I'd glimpsed two of the dwarfs the night before, but I was in no hurry to send the man off on their trail. In addition, I wasn't sure how seriously to take his words. That said, I had been to Trotsky's house myself, twice, once on a school trip and once with my parents, and could see why he got so worked up. It was the sort of place that made you mistrust everyone, and those watchtowers didn't even serve their purpose since Trotsky's assassin walked in through the door in a thick overcoat, sweating profusely in the Mexican summer yet raising no suspicion, and along with the towers I remembered the rows of empty hutches in the garden, their green wooden frames and rusty wire mesh, in which Trotsky kept his pet chickens and rabbits, rising early each morning to tend to them, an activity that according to his wife brought him tremendous calm. One could trust rabbits and chickens more than any human being, you didn't have to be a revolutionary to know that. And for several moments I was back at the house on Viena in Coyoacán, there in the garden with its variants of green, including the cacti Trotsky had collected on various expeditions and carried back and planted himself. As I sat there on the bench in the garden I tried to work out, or at least fathom, the continuum between this secluded place and the present, aware that Trotsky was murdered before the beginning of the Cold War, before Soviet circuses toured Mexico, before an age when cosmonauts were catapulted into space, carving paths in the firmament while equipped with sleeping masks to shield them from a succession of sunrises in orbit, in other words, before the Soviet Union of my imagination.

I was startled from my thoughts by the abrupt appearance of the merman, summoned, I couldn't help feeling, by my reverie. With a grunt of acknowledgment he sat down, clutching his cold bottle of Negra Modelo, his breathing altered and irregular, the rhythm of a system that had overheated and was still cooling down. I couldn't imagine what had kept him away until now, the clock read 10:40, but refrained from asking. As soon as he'd settled in and taken a few sips of beer I told him about the dwarfs, how I'd glimpsed them under the full moon after we'd said good night, had he seen this moon, I asked, hanging over the beach in dejected incandescence, and as best I could I described the scene I had witnessed, the tiny duo, the sound of their language, the way they'd pointed up at the sky and then wandered off. But the merman's face remained impassive, even when I repeated that the figures were almost definitely two of the Ukrainian dwarfs, full-moon vivid, he simply wasn't impressed, in fact he began to yawn and his hands started to undress his beer, peeling off the label that was draped across the bottle's chest like a sash. Perhaps for him it was a matter of little consequence and in his country the news was full of such stories of defection and reappearance, who was to know, and that night he seemed distracted, for the first time since we'd met his eyes weren't fastened on me and kept roaming the bar.

We'd just replenished our drinks, or rather the waiter had brought us two more, when the overhead lamps flickered, first once and then several times more and then, much to the dismay of everyone present, they went out altogether, plunging the palapa into night, the real night we'd been ignoring. The music stopped too. One of the barmen tapped a spoon against the side of a glass and called for silence. Silence took a while to achieve, but once most of the voices had dropped off he announced there'd been a short circuit, but not to worry—we just had to wait for the Zipolite electrician to arrive, and soon all would be back to normal.

It occurred to me to tell the merman about the time of the storm. The dash through the typewriter rain. The Covadonga. Julián and his shadow play. Once I'd finished we sat listening to the restlessness of people around us whose revelry had lost its momentum, and after fifteen minutes or so the lamps came back on, tentative at first and then full glow, and the light revealed an intriguing sight: the merman on the edge of his seat, a feverish look in his eyes, so fevered, clammy, and intense, I worried for an instant he'd been bitten by a malarial mosquito. Before I could ask whether something was wrong, though I sensed it wasn't, he leaned forward and took my face between his hands and brought it gently to his. There and then the language stopped, and without finishing our drinks we rose and found the nearest way out of the palapa, into shadow and across more shadow while somewhere in the distance a lantern gave off an orangey glow and the sea roared in my ears as if I could reach out and run my fingers through the water, and more than ever I sensed that in Zipolite anything was possible. Once in my hammock his strong hands grabbed at my clothes and began pawing at my body, the same pair of hands that had patted and moistened and shaped the sand, but also, how could I forget, the same hand that had pounded the fly. A current surged through me as though the ocean and its waves had entered, an oceanic force pushing farther and farther in, and the merman murmured something in his language, and I in mine, as the hammock sagged closer to the sand, its cords stretching and threatening to unravel, a drop in pressure, a rise in pressure, a riding of the waves, a journey to the seabed, a thrust back up to the surface, and something within me coiled tighter and tighter until it could coil no more and then sprang undone. The merman remained with me until the early hours of the morning, when the beach was starting to awaken. I watched him rise from the hammock, slip on his clothes and sandals, and after a final kiss he crept off, just as the sky began to soften from bruised purple to blue. In his canto to the ocean Lautréamont calls it a vast bruise on the body of the earth, yet I couldn't help feeling as though the bruise was left, rather, on those who came into contact with the ocean, and not the ocean itself.

MORNING TOSSES NIGHT'S ACTIONS AND ASSUMPTIONS out the window, and the morning light confirmed that the merman was gone, evaporated like the top layer of mist from a dream. After a visit to El Cósmico, the coffee as bitter as the previous day, I roamed the shore. There were fewer tourists than usual; large swaths lay empty apart from clumps of seaweed and the occasional bird prodding the ground with its beak. And where were the shells, I asked myself, I couldn't understand why Zipolite wasn't studded with nacre, hardly any ornamentation beyond the glitter of the sand itself, and only in a certain light. And what about the creatures within shells, surely there should be more of those too, creatures who lived half exposed and half secluded, the hidden half lost in its own geometry, tenanted shells and untenanted, cast off by waves or wily predators, and in my overcaffeinated state I envisioned the merman as one of their human equivalents, a creature with a conflicted relationship to the sun who sought at certain hours to retreat.

In the evening I sat at our table and faced the empty chair. I caught the waiter looking over, intrigued to see me on my own. But the merman did not show up, not at ten or eleven or midnight. He was probably on his way home, soaring over the ocean, back to his unnamed country, with all my stories. At midnight I returned to the palapa. In the distance I saw the beachcombers. And the ocean that threatened to devour everything in its sight. An emptiness, expanding. I returned to the bar and spent the last of my money on a cocktail, keeping a futile eye on the corner from where the merman would usually emerge, his serious face beside a column, but no, he'd been removed from the beach's conversation. The space filled with vagabonds but I no longer felt part of it. Even the dwarfs had ceased to concern me. And with the merman gone, the buffer, the ballast, was stripped from my senses, allowing for a gloomy monotony to set in. I felt the ocean intruding, salt water in what I drank, sandy grains in what I ate, a rippling in most surfaces. The shoreline ran through every face, destroying some, enhancing others. Someone offered me their joint. I took a few drags and passed it on . . . Beach of the Dead, the name rang in my ears, Beach of the Dead . . . Well, all manner of things came to die here. That night I longed for one of Tomás's white pills but discovered he'd taken his bag with him, nothing left but the shed cocoon of his hammock.

I woke up earlier than usual and walked on autopilot over to El Cósmico, the beach's power source, I'd concluded, rather than its center. Oddly enough, I was the only customer. The young girl wasn't there that day, only her mother. After she brought me my coffee I asked what she thought had happened to the Zapotec girls, why they had run into the water if they knew they couldn't swim. Sometimes people are seized by a mad impulse, the woman replied immediately, an impulse that seems to come from nowhere, that's what happened to these girls. They were walking along hoping to sell their jewelry when some mysterious impulse grabbed hold of the four of them and they threw off their clothes and ran into the ocean. The same thing happened to the drowned poet: he too was seized by an impulse no one could understand.

What drowned poet? I asked with a little trepidation. Oh, that was last year, it's old news now. The man, well, they said he wrote verses though there's no bookstore here to prove it, he ate and drank a lot at lunch and then entered the water and swam very far out and began to wave and wave. People who saw him from the shore couldn't tell whether he was saying goodbye or asking for help; his friends had apparently warned him of the dangerous tide so it's not as if he was unaware of the danger. In any case, after waving he soon disappeared into the waves and one hour later the fishermen found him farther along the beach. They hauled him out and laid him on the sand, everyone ran over to have a look, and the fishermen's wives rested his head on a bed of herbs and one of them recited a prayer. He looked peaceful, and not bloated at all, and three children from the village laid flowers and leaves on his body. Usually when people drown they're carried off without ceremony, but on this occasion there was a beautiful scene, yes, it was beautiful, and we were all part of the stranger's farewell. There hadn't been much sun that morning, the day had started overcast, that's what happens when someone is going to die, and then came this man who swam out too far, well, it seems no one will ever know what his intentions were, but it happened here, not far from El Cósmico.

The woman seemed to revel in tragic stories, a kind of fascination with misfortune. I drew my eyes away from the gold tooth but there was no ignoring her voice, as melodious and disquieting as recorded birdsong. My appetite more or less dashed, I asked for the bill. As I walked along the shore speculating where the merman might be found that morning, and, more importantly, whether I'd once more be filled with longing or whether something had been laid to rest, I happened to spot the hut. There it sat, blue and peculiar, a few meters from the ocean. I tried to recall its last location, and how this might be indicative of recent movements of the tide. It always looked so motionless, an oversized hermit crab hoping to go unnoticed, and I was about to move my gaze onward when the door sprang open and out stepped Tomás. Squinting in the sunlight, he did a morning stretch before moving aside for an older woman behind him. The lifeguard, presumably. Even at a distance I could see her sharp cheekbones and long lashes, her thick eyebrows ancillary to a mane of black hair. She wore an old-fashioned bathing suit with a low neckline and a short flared skirt. I would've never imagined her profession was saving drowners. Where had she been on the days of the Zapotec girls and the poet?

Overcome with curiosity I began to follow, but my attention was soon drawn away by loud male voices shouting to each other at the water's edge. Two *lanchas* were being pushed off into the sea. They'd rarely congregate here, usually just howl past over pleated sheets of water, and halt farther down the beach at a spot with fewer sunbathers. Yet that morning they'd come ashore here. And these boats, though peeling, were both painted a deep regal blue, I noticed, as one of the men waded out and threw a coiled rope into the second boat, and yelled a command, informing the boat operator, whose name appeared to be Gustavo, of two gringas who wanted to be taken on an excursion to a neighboring beach. The man seemed to protest. The other man insisted. The one named Gustavo gave in. His voice wasn't noteworthy but his bathing trunks certainly were: green, high-waisted, with a blue stripe down the side. With something like vertigo I looked up at the face, half refuged in the shade of a cap. Gustavo. The merman was a *lanchero* named Gustavo. No, it couldn't be. And yet my eyes were telling me it was.

So this was how he spent his days, half on land, half on water. He hadn't seen me, was too busy revving the motor in preparation for passengers, his arms now looking plump rather than muscled in the Pumas T-shirt stretched tightly over his chest. Was it definitely him, well, maybe not, I was starting to think, until he removed his cap to wipe the sweat from his brow and revealed an unequivocal face. His features were much more rounded than they appeared at night. Unlike the afternoon of the sandcastle, the sun now erased all Slavic accents and geometry. There he was, Gustavo, aka the merman, unsteady on his feet as his blue boat rocked from side to side. The motor emitted its loud rat-tat-tat, though to my ears the sounds merged into one long whoosh as the vessel and its operator, now crouching over the motor, careered out into the open sea, carving a big V into the waves.

The rest of the afternoon passed by in a haze. I found a spot beneath a palm tree and felt time surge upward through its base. I chose a young palm, its fronds green to the tip as opposed to the others that tapered into yellow. In general I preferred plants with branches, they were more expressive, but I couldn't help feeling affection for these armless trees, simply a long trunk ending in fireworks of leaves. Gusts of wind stirred up the sand, blowing two plastic cups down the shore. A group of young men set up a volleyball net and began their game. One of the dogs came to scratch at his fleas beside me. Every now and then I'd check the horizon but no more boats, no motors sounding in the distance. Green flag: calm water. All so calm and harmonious, and yet I could feel the distress of the landscape. The beach didn't want to hold these people, it didn't want to be a stage, it wanted to go back to being a pure arrangement of stock motifs. Sitting there against the base of the palm tree, I could perceive a defeated silence beneath the layers of noise and activity.

Tomás materialized in the evening as I stood in a corner of the palapa wrapping a skirt around my waist. He was no longer accompanied by the black-maned woman yet smelled faintly of rotting algae. Where had I been all day, he asked, he'd been looking for me everywhere. Zigzagging, I replied, up and down the shore. I see, he said, as if zigzagging were the most natural form of movement, and asked whether I'd like to join him at a bonfire. I accepted without hesitation: the moment had come for other company and distraction.

Once we'd located his bonfire, one of many, a ficry neck-
lace along the beach, we took our place in the ring of people. Two Swedish tourists, a young man from Malmö with
a pencil mustache and a young woman with a Hello Kitty
tattoo on her forearm, stoked the wood and then set to
work fashioning a four-inch joint. They had just been to Es-
cobilla to watch the sea turtles lay their eggs, they said, and
swore that nothing in life would match the experience. The
joint was passed around. Someone else hadn't seen any turtles, but mentioned a pair of broken dentures they'd found
at the foot of a tree. One less treasure for the beachcombers.
A Chilean youth sat down among us; he was very tall and
had a cataract in one eye, visible in the light of the flames.
Someone should paint the landscape of your cataract, the
Swede said in seriousness as the joint neared its end.

I tried to enter the scene but a deep melancholy of the
kind that sometimes freights sunset had begun to close in.
I still found it hard to process what I had seen that day.
Gustavo. Local, rather than from overseas. Spanish, rather
than some unfathomable tongue. But after a drag on the
joint, maybe two, I slowly began to convince myself that
perhaps I had imagined it, somehow the act of imagining
seemed more likely than the extravagant vision I'd seen,
and after another drag in the presence of the crackling fire
that moved the light back and forth across people's faces,
I decided it was possible, very possible, that my eyes had
deceived me. Yet it remained difficult to connect with the

good humor, in fact I had no desire to, I wasn't cut out for bonfires and never had been, bonfires or picnics, actually, I could only vaguely see the allure, had never liked the idea of sitting casually and lazily around a center. I stared into the fire, at the different fragments of driftwood, I stared at the grains of sand clinging to my feet and my skirt, and as if under the spell of the stage magician who asks us to imagine an object's inner life, I began to feel that every little thing was in some way animate, harbored its own anxieties and desires that existed alongside our own, and that these grains of sand, for instance, were hoping to be transported elsewhere, if they just hung on long enough to my feet and my skirt they'd be taken to new places, could begin a new life, a better life, far from Zipolite. At least the flames no longer reminded me of the fire-eaters, in fact few sights now reminded me of the city, that was a lifetime ago, or rather a parallel life, of another Luisa who lived in La Roma, housed, schooled, and parented, and I preferred to confine my thoughts to the present. Yet before long, they were thrown back to the city.

I was thinking about how one never sees the same flame twice, each form unique and never to be repeated, in the same way that a person is never repeated, nor does a person ever repeat themselves in the exact same way at any two given moments, when our circle widened for a couple who joined us, the young man in a green T-shirt and the young woman in a tank top that showed the outline of her nipples. As soon as their faces became visible I knew I had seen them before. I asked where they were from. California, they replied, they'd just arrived in Zipolite that night. The girl adjusted the strap on one of her sandals.

You're from the Burroughs apartment, I said.
What?
From the day we went to see the place where Burroughs . . .
Who's he?
William Burroughs.
We don't know him.
Yes, on Monterrey.
We've only been to Mexico City and Oaxaca.
Monterrey Street, in the city.

I tried to further explain but the girl hissed and the boy had eyes for nothing but the joint. But . . . No, they had arrived that night and had never met my friend Burroughs, they said again, their voices rising a note. I looked to Tomás, who had been following our exchange, but instead of insisting on my behalf he leaned forward and placed a shell on my head, a rather flattish one, and clasped his hands into the shape of a gun.

Pow! he cried, as the boy from Malmö laughed uneasily.

I closed my eyes to him and to the scene, imagining for a brief moment a spider positioned at four o'clock on her web. When I reopened them Tomás was taking aim a second time, grinning in a way that lacked all playfulness.

Something made me look up.

The shell slid off as I raised my head.

And saw my father.

Or at least a man who looked incredibly similar to my father.

Through the quivering flames, a face familiar, beloved.

Without a word he glanced at me, his expression impossible to read, and then walked away.

I grabbed Tomás's arm.
My father is here!
The sideshow grin quickly fell.
You're hallucinating.
No, I really saw my father.
Where?
I don't know—he looked at me and walked off.
Why would he come all this way, look at you, and walk off?
I shook my head.
First you see the dwarfs, now you see your father!

The others laughed.

I'm sure it was him.

In that case, go find him and bring him back so you can introduce us.

The sounds of the ocean swelled to a deafening clamor, senses thrown into relief as I ran from the fire and into the night, but my nerves drove me to the wrong palapa, where I came face-to-face with a man with bloodshot eyes. He leapt out of his hammock and brandished a bottle in the air, several more scattered on the sand, and yelled ¿*Sí?* in a hoarse and wretched voice.

At my palapa there was no one, nor at the ones nearby, an eerie absence, everywhere, as if apart from the drunkard everyone had decided to vanish. The only beings I saw, in the distance, were the bowed silhouettes of the beachcombers absorbed in their mission, indifferent to any dramas unfolding on the beach.

Back at the bonfire Tomás was waiting. He took hold of my arm and pulled me toward the shoreline. Even in the dark I could see, or rather sense, his expression, somewhere between panic and anger. They're here, he muttered, they're here.

What do you mean? I asked, though I knew, at least partly, what he meant.

Still gripping my arm, he pointed to an inky spot that lay in the indeterminate space between sea and bonfire. And there stood my father, for now I was certain it was him, and beside him a man in a beret who looked like Tomás but older, and farther to the right, several other men, I was too bewildered to count, some in uniform and others in civilian dress. Everyone was turned in our direction, with not a smile between them. The ocean holds the most everlasting night of all, in its depth night is perpetual, a thick and total darkness untouched by the sun, light can penetrate water but only so far, and much of the ocean remains forever opaque; at thirty meters, night lasts nineteen hours, at forty-five meters, night is unrelenting for all but fifteen minutes of a solar day, and those fifteen minutes offer a fleeting twilight, nothing more.

My father approached, his gait tired and disheveled. *Why, Luisa?*

A question for which I had no answer.

I SLEEPWALKED THROUGH IT ALL, PATERNAL ORDERS and long-range maternal ones, two searchlights trained on me, and was too tired to have any thoughts of my own, relieved to have my trip, what was left of it, in someone else's hands, no more decisions, no more nights in the hammock, I would be fed and looked after and not have to worry. Have you eaten? my father had asked, before locating a *fonda* that agreed to serve food at midnight. Four painted blue chairs and a square table were set out on the sand, meters from the ocean. The waves of the Pacific were tall, white, electric. I sat across from Tomás, and our fathers across from each other. An oil lamp was placed at the center of the table, our faces turned into masks. My father requested a plate of potato tacos for me, and some rice. The others had shrimp and fish. Tomás ordered a Corona and then three more, making loud suctioning sounds each time he drank, his father watching him out of the corner of his eye.

After our dinner, during which very few words were spoken, I fetched my bag from the palapa. The overhead lamp glowed brightly but there was still no one to be seen. In the meantime my father had asked to use the phone in the *fonda* to call my mother and tell her I had been found. She wanted to speak to me, but they got cut off and it had been impossible to reestablish the connection.

A pleasure to meet you, Mr. Román said to my father, extending his hand, I'm glad we found what we were looking for. He then said a more formal goodbye to the driver and the policemen. Everyone lingered for a few moments under a cloud of *This is it?* until one of the policemen turned away. As for the farewell with Tomás, it was as halfhearted as what had come before. At most it was one half cleaved in two, left there in the sands of Zipolite. And when he said, You knew this would happen, you knew, what could I say but that of course I hadn't, I never expected anyone to come looking for me, the thought hadn't even crossed my mind, and those were my last words to him before my father and I climbed into the car.

The driver took us down unlit roads framed by unidentifiable foliage, the night creatures stopping in their tracks as we passed, and I thought back on the Baudelaire poem and what it seemed to say, how to imagine travel is probably better than actually traveling since no journey can ever satisfy human desire; as soon as one sets out, fantasies get tangled in the rigging and dark birds of doubt begin their circling overhead.

The roads grew less discernible, given substance by nothing but the lights of our car, and although there weren't any visual indications I sensed from the air and the murky forms that we were driving away from the coast, inland. My father seemed on the verge of sleep and I too was drifting off when we turned into a road that turned into a street that turned into a plaza and at the far end of the plaza the driver came to a halt in front of a colonial building.

Our hotel, a former sixteenth-century convent with carved doors, high ceilings, and muscular candelabra, was called Parador del Mar. A man clearly roused from slumber showed us to our room, trudging down the corridor as if his ankles were in chains. Parallel beds at opposite ends, a wooden chest holding a television, two armchairs on either side of a tiled fireplace, a wardrobe with thick confessional doors. I took it in without feeling part of it. My father settled into one armchair and I into the other, the fireplace between us a safe referee. The room was chilly, all stone and shadow, the ceiling traversed by wooden beams. I glanced at the pile of logs by the fireplace but feared they'd be full of spiders. At first we sat without speaking, each locked into our thoughts, into the forked path of recent experience. But I wouldn't be able to rest until I'd asked the question.

How did you find me?
It's a long story.
I'm ready.
Tomorrow . . . I don't have the energy. This is the first moment I can relax since leaving home. You must be tired too. When did you leave?
It feels like a long time ago.
I just want to know how you found me.
Let's go to sleep now. We'll speak tomorrow, he said, and closed his eyes.

The distance to his bed was too great, I imagined, as was the thought of any further conversation, and as I watched my father drifting off, a man in an armchair who looked older and wearier than his fifty-six years, I was overcome by emotion, how could I not be, when I considered how the whole time I'd been wandering Zipolite fixated on matters that, looking back, had already diminished in importance, my father had been wandering another Oaxaca with one objective in mind. After who knows how many days it had been met, whereas my objective, well, it was harder to say where it stood in the spectrum of fulfillment, but I wasn't going to worry about that now, the bed was calling, a solid steady four-poster that wouldn't sway or engulf or serve as a landing strip for large whirring insects, and after removing my shoes I switched off the lamps but even then I could see my father's silhouette there in the armchair thanks to the illumination seeping in from the plaza. And it was a thoroughly calming sight.

Breakfast was served in the courtyard under cascades of fuchsia bougainvillea. During my time by the sea I'd almost forgotten the generosity of flowers, as well as the sensation of being enclosed by architecture. After ordering every vegetarian item on the menu—*huitlacoche* crepes, *quesillo a la plancha*, fried potatoes, fried tomatoes, fried nopales, quesadillas—my father embarked, finally, on a chronicle of his search. More than once while he spoke my hunger withdrew, but each time I'd pause and lay down my fork he would say, Eat, Luisa, otherwise I won't continue, although he too paused often, either trying to recall a certain detail—he seemed to leave out very few— or the right sequence of events or, at moments, because it was all too much. And while he spoke a bird kept trilling overhead, insistent yet invisible in the bougainvillea, and each time I felt perturbed I would look up and try to find this bird, the sight of which might have granted some solace, but it chose to remain hidden, sharing nothing but its voice, which punctuated my father's speech as he described the many highs and lows of his journey, the moments of doubt, and my mother's insistence that he not give up.

When you didn't come home from school that day, he began, I wasn't worried at first. Your mother said you had gone over to Marcela's house to work on a history project. It was only when you hadn't returned by dinnertime that we grew anxious, but whenever we tried calling Marcela's number it was busy. So we drove all the way to her house, beyond Tlalpan. No one answered when we rang the bell so I called out your name, then Marcela's. Eventually Marcela's stepfather opened and wasn't particularly friendly. He said he hadn't seen you in weeks and had no idea where you were, and closed the door in our faces . . . But just as we were about to leave the door flew back open. It was Marcela, in her nightgown, and she yelled out four words—*She's with Tomás Román*—before being pulled back inside.

We recalled you had been out with this character a few times, and had always returned home later than promised. You'd also mentioned to your mother that he'd dropped out of school. But in the same conversation you had supplied her with a useful bit of information: that his mother taught art at the school near the Ángel cinema. The next day we watched through a classroom window as a woman surrounded by her students gave shape to a spinning urn. We waited for what seemed like ages for the bell to ring and, once the students had left, introduced ourselves. Tomás's mother seemed startled and insisted she had no idea where her son was. Perhaps her husband would know more. She wrote down the address of his office and we drove over. The building had many cracks and hanging chunks of plaster—I told your mother to wait in the car. Juan Román's name was listed on a board in the lobby and I took the elevator up to the sixth or seventh floor. It was an odd place, with sad-looking offices along a corridor, first a Cuban travel agency, then the deserted headquarters of a defunct magazine called *Calambres*, and then an office with a plaque that said RAMÍREZ Y ROMÁN. When I knocked no one answered but the door was open so I went in. The space looked a little forsaken, the windowpanes covered in muck, diplomas crooked on the walls, the water cooler empty.

Just as I was about to leave a man entered through a side door. He was wearing a beret and said his name, Juan Román. Perhaps it was my imagination but he seemed nervous; I couldn't help thinking his wife must have called in advance. He offered me a chair and then spoke one word: *Oaxaca*. He said his son went several times a year and it was his favorite place. He couldn't guarantee you would be

there but his guess was that his son was in Oaxaca, probably somewhere on the coast. I began to feel dizzy and
asked for a glass of water. Mr. Román reminded me the
cooler was empty. I asked him to accompany me to the
travel agency down the corridor, where a woman sat amid
posters of tropical destinations. She was reading *Reader's
Digest* but put it down when we entered. I inquired into
flights to Oaxaca. She said there was one early that evening. I said I wanted to buy two tickets. Mr. Román inter
rupted and said he was scared of flying. He would take the
train and meet me there in two days' time, at the main café
in the square, at five.

Before I set out for the airport I remembered an old ac-
quaintance from years past, someone for whom I once
wrote a letter of recommendation; after a failed career
in academia he entered politics and was recently elected
governor of Oaxaca. I found his card and called him. Not
only did the man promise to help me find you, he said
he would send someone to collect me at the airport and
bring me to my hotel, and not only that, he was going
to assign several police officers and a car. He would also
send word across the state. And should I think of anything else, I must let him know. That is Mexican generosity, Luisa, state-level.

Your mother helped me pack. We decided she should stay
and wait at home, in case you called or returned. I don't

remember much of the flight except that I tried to nap and couldn't. At the airport in Oaxaca there was someone waiting for me, a man holding a placard with my name misspelled in black letters. After dropping off my bag at the hotel he drove me to the town hall to meet Licenciado Augusto Ardilla, yes, that was his name, who was the governor's secretary. He asked whether I had any pictures of you. Fortunately I had one in my wallet, taken on your birthday last year. He studied it and then asked whether I had one of the so-called young man. I said no, I had never met him. So I described his father. Ardilla wrote down the information with a Montblanc and then picked up the phone and rang what turned out to be the chief of police of the state of Oaxaca, ordering him to notify his men. He studied your picture and described you. There's just one thing, I told him once he hung up. If your men should find them, please make sure they treat my daughter with respect. Don't worry, he said, my men are violent only when circumstances call for it. After this efficient exchange at the town hall, I had dinner at a café in the zócalo. I sat at a table facing out in order to watch the people walking past, hoping that one of the faces that crossed in the twilight might belong to you.

The next morning over breakfast I had an idea: the main bus terminal. Perhaps you had reserved tickets to Puerto Escondido or somewhere else along the coast. Every step of mine would now be shadowed by others—Ardilla had assigned two judicial policemen with instructions to follow me wherever I went, taciturn types who spoke only when spoken to. The driver, Abraham Reyes, was more affable. All three men were waiting for me in the lobby. At the bus terminal I asked an old man at the ticket counter whether I could see a list of the passengers who'd bought tickets to Puerto Escondido over the past two days. At first he regarded me with suspicion. I explained I was looking for my daughter. At the top of the second page there was the name Tómas. Someone named Tomás had purchased two tickets for the next bus to Puerto Escondido, leaving at 11:30 that morning. The policemen suggested I not show myself on the grounds you might hide if you saw me. Passengers began to arrive, mostly Mexicans and a few tourists too. I checked the alley where the parked buses sat warming their engines but you weren't on any of them. And then the bus filled up, every seat taken, including the two reserved for Tomás. Back at the plaza I treated my companions to lunch.

As we sat eating, a man with a notebook approached and said I looked familiar, that I had the face of someone famous but he couldn't quite place the name . . . And that I must be very famous indeed if the governor had lent me two policemen and a chauffeur. He asked my name and the reason for my trip. Seeing a window for comic relief, I gave him the name of a well-known and rather pompous novelist, well, you know who. The man's eyes grew wide,

and he then asked the reason for my trip. I told him to return the next day and I would give him an answer. And off
he went with his notebook, before I had the chance to ask
what paper he wrote for.

Despite this brief moment of comedy, my optimism
was on the wane. The possibility of finding you seemed
to grow slimmer with every passing hour. I called your
mother and said I was starting to lose hope. I would fly
back tomorrow evening, after seeing Mr. Román. But she
insisted I stay on and not give up. If I didn't look for you,
who would, and did we really want to be sitting at home
waiting for the phone or the bell to ring? We couldn't leave
your fate in the hands of others. After breakfast the following day I returned to the terminal to examine the passengers boarding for Puerto Escondido. Only one stood
out, a young blond woman carrying a suitcase she could
barely lift. Her resemblance to the daughter of a colleague
of mine was so great that I went up and asked whether
she was Naira Blau from Munich, to which she replied in
a French accent that no, she had never heard of this Naira
Blau, but could I please help with her suitcase. After assisting her onto her bus I showed her your photograph and
asked that should she see you anywhere, to please tell you
to call home at once.

Abraham and the two policemen were waiting in the hotel
lobby. We agreed to meet in two hours at the main café in

the zócalo. In view of the long and difficult journey ahead, Abraham would go to the ministry and exchange his Ford for something sturdier.

Mr. Román was already at the café, armed with his beret and a copy of *unomásuno*. He stared at me fixedly. I sensed he knew more than he let on. After the waiter brought our coffees he said he'd had an idea. San José del Pacífico. Up on the sierra. Its highest point. He said his son loved the place for the view and the mushrooms . . . And if we don't find them? Then we'll drive on to the coast.

He gave a start when Abraham and the two policemen walked up to our table. I explained that these men would be accompanying us. Abraham held up a set of keys and said we now had a nice red station wagon. Half an hour later we were on the highway, Abraham and I in the front, and Mr. Román in the back with the two policemen. Beyond the window lay a theater of green, mainly rocks colonized by moss, you must have seen them too, but Mr. Román asked question after question, making it impossible for me to appreciate the view, and didn't react when fragments of road broke off and plunged into the ravine alongside us. It is, after all, one of the most dazzling and treacherous highways in the world . . . Only when Abraham pointed up at a peak in the distance, a miniature triangle set against an intense blue sky, and said that was our destination, did Mr. Román fall silent.

Along some stretches the road was too narrow for two cars to pass at once. An abyss with tall trees loomed on either side. Abraham tackled every curve as our station wagon climbed the winding road, deciduous trees giving way to pines. After nearly an hour we reached San José del Pacífico. A thick blanket of fog enveloped the car as we entered the tiny rudimentary village devoid of signs and shops. The place is called San José del Pacífico because one can in principle see the Pacific from its peak. On one side the ocean, on the other the Gulf of Mexico. But that day I couldn't see to the end of the road. Everyone got out to stretch their legs. A stray dog limped past, and as I watched the fog swallow its scrawny body I realized there was no promise, no trace, of you in this village that floated high above the rest of the world. The thought was soon reinforced by a curious vision: four men in hats and sarapes emerging from the mist, inching toward me along the pebbled road past the skeleton of a tree, travelers to and from some unknown destination for whom San José del Pacífico was no stranger than any of the other villages they crossed. The men's hats were worn low, hiding their faces almost entirely, and even more than the solitary dog, the image of these men captured the phantasmal atmosphere of small Mexican mountain villages that belong more to the clouds than the earth.

• • •

Let's try Pochutla, Abraham Reyes proposed when everyone had returned to the car. It's a much larger town, he said,
and is on the way to the coast. We rolled down our windows to let in some mountain air. A vehicle came toward
us. The driver stuck out his head to warn of two bridges up
ahead, both on the verge of collapse. He said to avoid them
if we could. Abraham thanked him and continued. We'd
gone too far to turn back; we had to take our chances.

The condition of the first bridge was certainly ominous, a
rotting wooden serpent stretched over a drop that would
scare a dragon. The policemen crossed themselves as our
car rolled onto it. A couple of stones and what looked like
a plank tumbled off one side. Up and down we bounced, as
if the bridge were assessing our weight, deciding whether
to grant us passage or let us plummet. I had to force my
gaze away from the window. Once we were a few feet away
from safety Abraham stepped on the accelerator and we
flew over the final stretch.

A kilometer later the second bridge appeared, even longer than the first. This one danced in the wind. It, too,
was made of rotting wood, weak and splintered even at
a distance. Half of its side rails were missing. Narrower
than its predecessor, every feature spoke betrayal. If we
turned around we would have to cross the first bridge
again. There we were, between Scylla and Charybdis, and
we hadn't even reached the ocean. Abraham let the car roll

forward as slowly as possible. No one said a word, in fact we hardly breathed, much less looked down—it was best not to acknowledge the immensity of the drop. A few eternal minutes later, we reached the other side.

But once the challenge of the bridges was overcome a new source of anxiety sprang up. Farther along the highway, we passed a brown car full of policemen speeding in the other direction. Not until the car was a dot on the horizon did Abraham say he thought he'd seen a teenage girl sitting inside, between the policemen. What did she look like? She was wearing an orange T-shirt and had black hair, he said.

Had it been you in the car and, if so, what were you doing there? Were you on your way to San José del Pacífico or beyond? And were you about to spend the night with these men, or what? I said we had to turn around immediately and follow the car. But no one agreed; it was unlikely it had been you, they argued, and even if it had been, we would never be able to catch up unless we flew over the sierra. We would try Pochutla first. And if you weren't there, Abraham promised, we could consider turning back. Yet the thought of turning around and retracing our route, bridges and all, hung over us like a very poor joke.

Upon arriving in Pochutla, a town perched halfway down the mountainside, we drove straight to see the head of the judicial police. The air had cooled during our descent and before going in I slipped on a pajama top under my shirt. The man looked as though he hadn't slept in days. His voice was feeble. So was his handshake. He told me he'd looked everywhere: cantinas, restaurants, even the prison. Your daughter's not here, he said, and never was. His assistant poured us each a mug of coffee. Well then, there's something I would like to know, I said, my mind still fixed on the brown car. What crimes are most frequent in your part of Oaxaca? Homicides, he said. Homicides. And who are the victims? Hard to say, you know violence in our country is so random. And after homicides what are the other leading causes of death? I asked. The surf on the coast is treacherous, he replied, people drown all the time . . . That undertow gets even the best of swimmers. The current is gentle in the morning and turns rough by the afternoon. Tourists drown every year, so do locals. I could feel my face blanching and drank down the rest of my coffee. But don't worry, he said, I'm sure your daughter is fine. I'll give you two more men. They will help you find her. He rang a bell and a short policeman walked in, trailed by a teenager in a Black Sabbath T-shirt. This is Juan Manuel and his assistant, Jaime. They will help you find your girl. As I shook hands with them I asked myself how these new additions could possibly bring me any closer to you.

Excuse me, but have you seen today's paper? Jaime asked. I said no. He ran out and returned with *El Sol de Oaxaca*, the local tabloid. Blazed across the front page in stark capital letters was the headline NOVELIST'S DAUGHTER KIDNAPPED BY YOUNG EUROPEAN. My mind raced over the people I had seen in Oaxaca during the past few days until I remembered the reporter who approached me at the café. I'd forgotten our appointment but someone else, evidently, had filled him in. The article was brief and laconic. It said that Mr. X, the famous novelist, had flown over from Mexico City to search for his daughter. The governor was lending him a hand. As for the young man in question, he had come to Mexico as a tourist and was known to prey on Mexican girls. His origins, the reporter speculated, were either Swiss or Austrian, and he could be easily identified by his pasty skin and jagged teeth.

Don't worry, Luisa, Mr. Román never saw the article. He was waiting in the car. As soon as I'd resumed my place in the passenger seat he said one word: *Zipolite*. Zipolite? Yes. I think we should drive straight there. But what about the brown car? It wasn't your daughter. And if it was, we will never find her by driving back over the sierra. I think he's right, Abraham Reyes echoed, let's try Zipolite. It's very popular with the young. Tomás loves it more than anywhere else in Oaxaca, Mr. Román added. That's what you said about San José del Pacífico, I replied.

And so it was that we finally arrived in Zipolite.

Even in the dark I could discern the long stretch of sand, the rocky headlands, the palm groves, the procession of bungalows and palapas, a cove at one end, towering sea cliffs at the other . . . I couldn't explain why, but for the first time I sensed we were getting close. Juan Manuel and Jaime advised me to seek out a certain Apolonio Cervantes, owner of a restaurant called El Árbol. He's like a German Shepherd, they said, nothing slips his attention and he keeps a file on every new presence.

Don't worry, Apolonio said when I introduced myself, we'll find your daughter. He grabbed a flashlight and asked the other men to remain at El Árbol, ordering his wife to bring them beer and dried shrimp.

As we began our walk down the beach Apolonio shined his flashlight into every face we passed, catching most by surprise. But none of them was yours. I was starting to feel desperate again. It was then that Abraham Reyes tapped me on the shoulder and pointed to a group of young people sitting around a bonfire. I crept over and in the ocher light I inspected every face. There was a boy with a thin mustache, and a girl with a tattoo, and a boy with pointy ears. And, next to him, a girl who resembled you.

Resembled me?

Well, yes, at that moment I wasn't certain of anything.

You seemed like another person. But one act does not
change the unity of a human being. When you turned
to look at me I didn't know what to say. So I walked
away. And I was standing by one of the palm trees trying to collect my thoughts when Mr. Román appeared
and asked whether I had seen you. They're over there,
he pointed. And, well, you know the rest. Your friend
Tomás was very defensive—I suppose he was aware that
you being seventeen and he being nineteen, he could be
charged with kidnapping a minor—and lost no time in
informing me, as if I didn't know already, that his father
was a lawyer. He said he was responsible for his actions
and his actions alone, and that it had been your idea to
run away.

I wasn't certain how to address that final comment and
now that my father had come to the end of his chronicle,
I realized I'd finished all the food in front of me, forks
and spoons laid across the plates, the mug and the glass,
even the jug, empty. And although he had reached the
end I sensed he didn't want me to speak, was afraid of
what I might say, and kept talking to fill the space. I felt
like reassuring him that *nothing had happened*, though of
course something *had* happened, however with someone
else, not with the person he assumed, and I now wished

to tell nothing but the truth, though I was no longer even sure what that was.

Once we'd left the hotel with its candelabra and bougain-villea and invisible bird we fell into a hush that lasted the entire taxi ride to the airport in Huatulco, as well as the plane journey home. The engines vibrated beneath our seats accompanied by a collateral roar outside, and with something close to vertigo I gazed down at the coastline, at a landscape similar to the one from which I'd recently withdrawn, the ocean's strips of blue like gradations in a color chart. I imagined Tomás perched on a boulder with his father and Mario, and the dogs dozing beneath a palm nearby, and Gustavo in his *lancha*, while the merman sat at our table in the bar—in the past twenty-four hours they'd split into separate entities—and the so-called life-guard in her pale blue hut, on the lookout for drowners and, beyond the hut, the sea-monstered waters I hadn't properly explored. And as I stared down, superimposing my aerial view onto my recollection of Tomás's drawing on the tablecloth, it occurred to me that shipwreck or no shipwreck, most voyages end in failure, and from the start we had set out for the wrong island, bypassing our destina-tion, or at least the destination we thought we were aiming for, although perhaps we never really were, since the real-ity must be that most boats destined for Kythera end up at the island opposite, or for every boat docked in Kythera there is one that travels onward to the smaller island whose geography also works against the machinations of Cupid. From the moment we set out, Tomás and I were heading toward Antikythera, armies of woodworm working their way through the mast, I thought to myself as the plane climbed higher and higher, the land and water below slipping away until finally eclipsed by a layer of cloud.

Why, Luisa? A question, an event, compressed into a fist, like a sentence compressed into an apostrophe that when released springs back to its original form. The divers from Symi went down looking for sponges and returned to the surface with bronze and marble castaways from another time. Compression and decompression of the lungs, history decompressed from a shipwreck, the movement of the ocean compressed into a sponge.

Upon disembarking from the plane in Mexico City we were greeted by a team of wheelchaired airport employees, part of a new scheme to offer employment to the disabled, well coiffed and ceremonial in their navy blue uniforms, smiling, waving, signaling the way to the luggage carousel. They were much friendlier than the upright individuals one usually encountered, and their waving arms segued into the rotating math instruments of the giant BACO sign on the Periférico. Towering over the flow of cars, the neon instruments continued to act out their functions, the scissors opening and closing, the compass going around and around, the ruler, the lead pencil, each taking their urban measurements, the lengths and widths of days, directions taken and untaken.

Before long our taxi became gridlocked in rush hour. From motion to slow motion to standstill, punctuated by a chorus of car horns: one would begin and the others would follow, repeating the same howl of impatience. And then along complicated loops and *laterales*, parallel side streets with indecipherable graffiti, language turning to dialect when straying from the main. My father had just rolled down his window—the air-conditioning wasn't working— when an army of Volkswagen Beetles closed in around us. They too struggled toward movement, these yellow and green dots between the longer vehicles, a Morse code of frustration from the road. Yet why should I be surprised, everything was rehyphenating, after all, that's what cities did, hyphenate and rehyphenate, but I couldn't help being amazed by how quickly my view had gone from crowded waves to automobiles; twenty-four hours ago I was still on the beach and now here I sat, returned to the center.

A little before six—released, finally, from the traffic's grip—our taxi pulled up outside our house. I brought our bags to the door and dropped them on the sidewalk while my father negotiated with the driver, who didn't have the correct change. I gazed at our doorbell and hesitated, then looked over at the house beside ours. The roof had been completed, the façade painted a shark gray. The crooked bars from before had been replaced by a forbidding metal door that now marked the entrance. Grilles had been set over the ground-floor windows and an electric fence buzzed over the outer wall. It seemed the workers had advanced in great strides while I was gone. Despite all the camaraderie, did their friendship last beyond each construction site, I wondered, or would it taper off once a house was built and they each moved on to new ones? Once something is constructed it is easier, perhaps, to walk away.

As I stood outside our house contemplating this important matter, I had the sense I was being watched. My mother's face, in an upstairs window. The pane was too clouded to gauge her expression but I could see the waxy circle of her face tilted down toward where I stood. I raised an arm and called out—the balcony door was open—but at that moment a truck full of old bicycles rumbled past, and while I debated whether to ring the bell or wait for my father to finish with the driver, I realized I wanted to prolong this moment for as long as possible, to remain in that suspended state between the voyage and the return. As I listened to the taxi drive off and my father's footsteps behind me, I decided I wouldn't tell them a thing, would not tell anyone, what had transpired, I would store it away in some deep chamber, yet even as I promised this to myself I knew it was futile, for regardless of how hard you try to keep memories at bay, after a while even bays erode, sandcastles collapse, and drowned mermaids resurface.

Acknowledgments

Many thanks to the John Simon Guggenheim Memorial
Foundation for its generous support.

And a great thank you to my editors Poppy Hampson and
Jonathan Lee, and to Suzanne Dean, Wah-Ming Chang,
Greg Clowes, and all the other fine people at Chatto & Win-
dus and Catapult who worked on this book. Thank you to
my agent, Anna Stein. And to Karolina Sutton and Mor-
gan Oppenheimer. And, of course, to Parisa Ebrahimi.

It would be impossible to list all the friends to whom I am
grateful, so I'll limit myself to those who formed part of
the ongoing dialogue: Josh Appignanesi, Devorah Baum,
Michael Bucknell, Andy Cooke, Vincent Dachy, Carlos
Fonseca, Iain Forsyth and Jane Pollard, Jennifer Higgie,
Stewart Home, Mary Horlock, Juliet Jacques, Andrew
Kidd, Darian Leader, Helder and Suzette Macedo, Claire
Nozières, Neil Porter, Simon Schama, Lorna Scott Fox.

Had this been memoir, my sister Eva would have featured
in nearly every city scene. But even in fiction, she is ever
present. Above all, I wish to thank Eva and my parents and
little Josephine, to whom this book is dedicated.